C000241611

Malleus Maleficarum,
maleficas ut earum hæresim,
ut phramea potentissima
conterens

The Shadow Rises

Witch-Hunter 1

K. S. Marsden

To Alison

Happy Reading

K. S. M

Printed by CreateSpace, an Amazon.com Company

Cover art: Sylermedia

Available from Amazon.com and other book stores

ISBN-13: 978-1499271607
ISBN-10: 1499271603

One

Hunter knocked back his cold, expensive beer. He was sitting alone at an open-air bar in the middle of Venice. It was late in the night, or at least it felt late - the days and nights seemed to take forever to tick past. The dark canal flickered with yellow lamp-light, along with new fragments of colour.

Hunter eyed the fairy lights that the new owner had strewn across the trellis beams, a cheap way to create a "youthful" environment. He didn't approve.

He looked around again, his gaze deadened as though he saw through the thin veil of these mortal amusements, and was not impressed.

Hunter Astley appeared to be a very normal guy, though one could never call him average. He ticked every box for the traditional English gent; in his mid-twenties, tall with black hair and classic good looks; he held an aura of charm and intelligence that was woven so appealingly about him; he had a confidence that was only partly to do with a large family fortune to his name.

Yet all this helped to distract people from looking too closely, to stop them noticing that scrutinising gaze and apathy to the mundane facts of life. Because under the veil, there were darker things to fear.

Hunter Astley was a witch-hunter.

Under the guidance of the Malleus Maleficarum Council, alongside other witch-hunters, Hunter worked tirelessly to eradicate witches and witchcraft, to prevent curses and black magic and to stop the witchkind gaining the hold and power over the unaware, ignorant world. The witches never stopped in their pursuit of power, so neither did Hunter and his fellow witch-hunters.

Except for now. Hunter was on holiday - against his own will, one might add. But the question was, when you know that evil magic is threatening everywhere beneath the surface, what does a witch-hunter do for a holiday?

Oh, he was bored. And in his bad mood, Hunter knew who to blame: James. Good old, annoying, interfering James Bennett. His colleague, who considered himself the brains of the operation, and was as loyal as he was irritating. The two of them had been working overtime since a big coop last hallowe'en, and last winter had been the busiest they had ever known the witchkind. The increased activity had taken more of a toll on Hunter of course. When considering the two of them, it was Hunter that was the man of action and James was his back-up, his background researcher.

James had taken it upon himself to insist that Hunter needed a break now that it was spring. Ok, things were calmer now, and ok, the last job had nearly killed him.

But only nearly, he was still alive. But his arguments had been ignored and Hunter had finally agreed to take a week's holiday, especially as James threatened to lock up all the open cases and divert current issues to the others.

Although, when Hunter agreed to stop work for a whole week, that didn't stop him sneaking into his own office to slip all the Venetian files into his suitcase before he left. Not that it had been much use. The damn files hadn't been kept up-to-date and he was chasing ghosts. And no, ghosts didn't exist.

A trio of young women sauntering past dragged his attention back to the present. They were all beautiful, but the tallest of the three was particularly striking.

Hunter noticed that his weren't the only eyes that watched them cross the room, so he was an average guy after all. He smiled at the idea, maybe James was right, maybe he could enjoy a holiday.

When he raised his gaze again, the girls had gone. Hunter drained the last of his beer and made his way over to the bar. He leant against it and waited for the barman. He noticed her perfume first, a fresh scent that contrasted sharply against the alcohol.

Hunter looked up to see one of the girls standing a few feet away. With her heels on, she was almost as tall as Hunter. Her dark brown hair was tied back, and there was a proud tilt to her jaw. Hunter appreciatively inventoried the slim waist and long legs.

As though sensing his inspection, the girl turned on her heels to face him. Her hazel eyes locked onto him, coolly assessing him in return. Apparently dissatisfied, the girl turned away again.

Hunter inwardly laughed, not even a word passed between them and he had been shunned. His poor ego. He ordered a drink, and as he waited for his beer to come, he caught a male voice – one whose accent didn't hide the waver of uncertainty.

"... let me buy you a drink."

Hunter turned to see a very smart, suited type, leaning in to the girl. His smile did nothing to disguise the fact his suggestion had been half a question. It almost reminded Hunter of how James was when he had to talk to beautiful girls. Honestly, Hunter felt a little sorry for men that floundered so easily.

He paid for his beer and found himself watching as the girl looked uncomfortable as the suit got closer. Her painted lips somehow managed to convey a pout and a sneer that spoke volumes against her silence.

The guy grew increasingly unsure at her stony silence and eventually slunk off.

Hunter smiled to himself, keen for the challenge. He moved towards her and finally spoke. "Scusi, signorina.."

Her eyes suddenly snapped onto him again, her frown increasing. "Scusa, non parlo l'italiano." She replied in perfect Italian.

Hunter smirked at her avoidance. "Great, neither do I! But it's good to know that you talk at all." He couldn't help but notice that she was even more beautiful close up. If one got past the fixed haughty glare, of course.

There was a twitch in her lips as though she fought down a smile. The woman turned to her friends. "Let's go." They obediently shifted away from the bar.

"Good night." She said to Hunter and, making no excuses, left.

Hunter watched her retreating figure. What a strange, beautiful girl.

Hunter stood nursing his beer for a quarter an hour, before giving in to his dull mood and heading home. He weighed up the desire for company tonight, there had been enough female eyes turned in his direction this evening, including the waitress at the restaurant earlier. But it felt like too much effort. No, he'd much rather go back to his apartment, have a night cap, and see when the next flight back to London was.

Although it was spring, it wasn't cold. The late night walk was actually pleasant as he moved away from the youthful hub and into the quieter streets. It was then that he heard a scuffle in the distance, followed by silence.

Hunter stopped, looking in the direction of the brief disturbance. It was most probably a cat, or something equally innocent. But that niggling feeling in his gut grew, calling to him. Damn it, was he getting withdrawal symptoms from work? Looking for trouble where there was none to be found? The utter silence made his senses tingle and his instincts kicked in and took over. He made his way quietly in the direction of the noise. Down a shadowed path to where a heavy door was ajar. Hunter stood against the gap and heard people moving inside, he began to see the weak light of candles as they were lit by two flitting figures.

Hunter reflexively lifted his hand to his throat, closing his fingers around the comfortable weight of the protective amulet. Next he knelt down and retrieved the small gun strapped to his calf, thankful that he had gone against his colleague's advice, that he had decided to remain armed.

Standing tall again, he slipped inside, pressing the door shut behind him. The large room was lit by a hundred candles - some witches were overly keen on the traditional touches. There was a makeshift altar, a long table covered with black silk, and a young woman strapped to it. She struggled sluggishly against her bonds, her breath fast and frightened. She was probably drugged, but at least she was alive. For now.

Hunter shifted around the edge of the room, keeping to the shadows. His eyes widened as he recognised the victim – the girl from the bar...

Her identity was confirmed when her two friends entered the circle of candlelight, bristling with excitement.

"P-please... please, you can't..."

Hunter could hear the girl's slurred pleas, her focus strengthening as those she considered friends came closer.

Hunter kept his own breathing low and steady, his gaze moving to a tall man with greying hair, although his face was unlined. He carried the knife, holding it up with reverence.

As he drew up to the altar, Hunter knew he had to act. There was no time to assess hidden dangers. He stepped into the light, trying to look as confident as possible. "Stop! Fermo!"

They all turned, shocked at the unwelcome man that had interrupted their ritual. Hunter rushed to speak before they caught up with the situation. "I charge you to stop. I am Hunter Astley, by the Malleus Constitution you will surrender now to my authority to be bound and registered. If you refuse to come quietly, I am empowered to take any means necessary."

Oh, it all sounded quite grand and official, and if he had had back up they might have turned themselves in harmlessly; but one Hunter against three put the odds in their favour.

"Assalire." Get him. The man ordered. "Subito!" Now! He barked as the two girls hesitated.

Ah, perhaps they were new to this game, Hunter thought, briefly giving him hope. But hope and desperation were put out of his mind as his body moved almost instinctively into action. He felt the charm about his neck heat up as it absorbed attacks from all three. He took aim with his gun and fired a single shot...

*****

The brown-haired girl woke up in a large bed with soft sheets, an early morning breeze rippling through the white cotton curtains and filling the room with cool and pleasant air.

"Good morning." Hunter said gently as he stood in the doorway, waiting for his guest to wake up. "How are you feeling?"

The girl sat up sharply, but then groaned, pressing her hand to her aching head. "Where am I?"

"Still in Venice, in my apartment. My name's Hunter by the way." He smiled politely. This was usually the part where people thanked him.

She frowned, a certain intelligent harshness returning now that she was fully awake. "Why? You

12

had no right to take me anywhere. What did you do, drug me?"

Hunter waited patiently for her to finish, a slight smirk at how easily people forget what was hard to believe. "It's nice to feel appreciated for saving your life," he replied calmly and innocently. "I'll put on some coffee, come on through when you're ready."

He walked into the main room, smiling as he did so.

The girl sat dazed for a moment, then slowly slid out of the covers and stood up. She was still in last night's clothes, the smell of smoke and alcohol clinging to them. She didn't hesitate for long and Hunter heard her bare feet padding into the very luxurious open plan apartment. She stood next to the sofa, watching Hunter suspiciously in the small kitchen.

"So last night was real? I mean, what happened, and why?"

Hunter didn't reply immediately, but brought through two cups of steaming coffee and invited his guest to sit down. "If you don't mind me asking, had you known those girls long?"

The girl shrugged, "A few days, they were at the same hotel as me. I was on holiday alone and they were friendly, inviting me out day and night. I thought they were ok."

"It was their job, to gain your confidence. But they were going to kill you, to sacrifice you, last night. They were witches." Hunter glanced up as he finished speaking, watching her carefully after this revelation.

"Witches?! As in 'fire burn and cauldron bubble'? You've got to be joking."

"No, I am completely serious," he replied with an apologetic smile. "Witches are real, and to be blunt, they're all black-hearted, evil... I'm sorry you got involved. If we were in England I could offer you something to erase the memory - but as it is..."

"Are there a lot of witches?"

Hunter shrugged. "Depends on what you mean by lots? There are too many in my opinion. If I tried to put a number on them, perhaps ten thousand worldwide." He paused to drink his coffee. "Does that surprise you?"

"I don't know; it's not something I've previously considered." The girl replied quickly and rather sharply. "But I suppose if you count all the fortune tellers and-"

"No." Hunter broke in with a rue smile. "All those harmless, normal people that play with the idea of using magic - they aren't witches. Witches are an entirely different breed of human, at least one parent has to be a witch; you can't become one by wanting it. And they don't waste their power telling fortunes at fairs either. Instead, they create illnesses and plagues; they torment victims with illusions and nightmares; they can bring storms, fires and floods. They do all this and more, for their own gain, or sometimes just because they enjoy it.

"Their powers are only limited by their strength - they gain a temporary boost from draining the life from victims; that is why they perform sacrifices, their thirst for power is insatiable. Sorry, I don't mean to frighten you."

The girl sat there quietly for quite a while, naturally taking time to comprehend all this. Finally she spoke with an obvious scepticism. "So... if those girls are witches, and I was the sacrifice - what does that make you?"

"A witch-hunter."

She raised a brow. "A witch-hunter named 'Hunter'? How very original."

Hunter sighed. "You're a very pleasant, friendly character, aren't you? So, you know about me, do I get to learn your name?"

"Sophie Murphy." She replied without hesitation. "What... what happened to the girls - I mean, the witches?"

Hunter paused. "The two female witches weren't very powerful creatures. They agreed to be bound. But the male witch that was in charge was executed on site."

"You killed him?" Sophie's voice shook.

It sounded bad, but people just didn't understand. "He wasn't willing to cooperate, I hope you don't mind." Hunter replied with a certain bite. Oh yes, he could act the hero and save her and get away unscathed, but he must do it without killing violent witches? Sure.

"So... bound? What does that mean?" Sophie asked more quietly, helpfully shifting the focus.

"Oh, it means they submitted to arrest. Then their powers are 'bound', effectively removed so they can never use them again. Then the witch serves time in prison, same as any convict." Hunter replied, giving the brief version of binding. The witch-hunter's handbook devoted about three dreary chapters on the subject. "You've got nothing to worry about from those girls, they're powerless and it may be a lifetime before they're free."

They were interrupted as the door flew open. A young man entered, slamming the door behind him before turning to glare at Hunter.

"You couldn't do it, could you? You couldn't go even two bloody days without looking for trouble?" A thick Yorkshire accent shouted out as he turned to throw down his coat and two bags in the kitchenette. "You call me up at 3 in the mornin', and it's me that's gotta fly out and clean up. I've already rang the Italian branch of the Council, we've got a meeting with 'em this afternoon - they're not happy, Hunter - you know the rules. You notify them if you're operating or hand it over to one of theirs."

Hunter sat back, appearing unfazed by this little outburst. When the young man had finished, he spoke quite coolly. "Sophie, this is my colleague, James Bennett. James, this is Sophie, the girl that would have been sacrificed by the time I had followed the proper lines of authority." Although he spoke calmly enough, there was a hardness in his tone.

James reined back his frustration as he held out his hand to shake Sophie's, while giving her an appraising glance. "Sure, spurred on by a bonny face." He muttered to no one in particular.

There was no denying the warning in Hunter's voice this time. "Just take her statement, Mr Bennett."

It took half an hour for James to take down everything Sophie had to say, then a further hour for her to answer his unending questions into every tiny detail. Finally he sat back, closing his notebook. "Right, thank you, Miss Murphy. I'll get this all typed and copied for the Council... ah, there's just one more thing."

He reached into his briefcase, and after ruffling through many stuffed-in papers he pulled out some sheets and handed them to Sophie. She took them hesitantly, glancing down at the thick paper covered in text.

"It's a non-disclosure contract," he explained, leaning over so that he could see the writing he already knew by heart. "I'm sure you can understand, it's to protect you and us from... well, other witches finding out, or idiot interference."

"He means the media and general stupidity of the human race," Hunter added as he hovered about the formal conversation.

Sophie looked between the two of them and back down to the contract. "So signing a piece of paper is supposed to guarantee my silence. I can see some flaws there."

"It legally and, ah, otherwise binds you to silence over the subject," James said seriously. "You will be unable to speak of it to anyone outside of the Malleus Maleficarum Council. Speaking of which, we'll organise you a contact for when you get back to England in case you want help, memory modification or the like."

Sophie continued to stare at the contract with an emotion resembling disgust. "And if I didn't sign it?"

Hunter leaned in, deadly serious. "We make sure you don't talk. As we said, it's for your own protection. I suggest you sign."

Sophie slowly picked up a pen and scrawled her name at the bottom of the page. James swiftly snatched it away from her and stuffed back in his briefcase. The three sat in silence for a few minutes before Hunter stepped up. "I'll see you out, Miss Murphy."

As he opened the front door for her, Sophie gazed up at him questioningly. "When do I see you again?"

"If everything goes to plan?" Hunter replied, leaning against the open door. "Never."

Two

Spring was warming to summer.

Amongst the rolling hills and the green pastures of the English countryside in the picturesque village of Little Hanting life went on as normal. It was a quiet, sleepy place, with fields of cows and rattling tractors. There were old stone houses built in clusters. The grandest of which was Astley Manor, set in a large estate. No one could remember a time when there wasn't the quiet, unobtrusive Astley family. George "Young" Astley VI had died unexpectedly five years ago, leaving the manor and the care of his widow in the hands of his then 20 year old son, known to all as Hunter.

And at this very moment, Hunter was seated in one of the large rooms, reading over a report written up by the ever-present James. Hunter sighed, even witch-hunting required paperwork in this crazy modern world - but thankfully Hunter could shift all that onto James' workload. He preferred the more active part of his job than this paperwork. And James did a tediously good and thorough job of it. James hovered over him, waiting for his response.

"Yes, that's all in order. Send a copy to the MMC." Hunter passed the thick sheaf of papers back.

The Malleus Maleficarum Council, the secret branch of witch-hunters under the pay of the crown; or MMC for short. All witch-hunters reported to them and were bound by their laws.

Hunter stood up and walked over to an old cabinet, one of those numerous antiques that filled his family's sprawling homestead. With a clink of glass he filled two glasses and passed one to James. "Here's to the end of that, then."

James took the drink. It had been an easy one this time, a single male witch in the East Midlands causing very localised trouble. He was comparatively weak and, faced with Hunter and James, he had succumbed to be bound from his magic and be registered with the MMC, to live quietly from now on. After the necessary jail time, of course.

"Excuse me, sir. There is a young lady here to see you." The mild voice came from the doorway. The family's long-serving butler waited for Hunter's attention. "A Miss Murphy. She is waiting in the sitting room."

"Thank you, Charles." Hunter replied, quite perplexed. Murphy? It sounded familiar. He exchanged a confused glance with James, before they rose together to meet the unknown guest.

A woman sat straight-backed on the settee, her long, dark brown hair casually tied back. She turned her head at their entrance and met them with a defiant stare.

"Mr Astley, Mr Bennett. I am Sophie Murphy. You may not remember me, but you came to my aid a couple of months ago - in Venice." The young woman spoke calmly and confidently and remained seated.

"Ah, Miss Murphy, of course." But Hunter frowned. "Forgive me, why are you here? The Council provided you with a contact?"

"Yes," Sophie replied. "But I didn't want to speak to a low-level pen-pusher. This won't take long, why don't you sit down."

Hunter gaped, speechless. He couldn't believe the girl's bloody cheek; inviting to sit down in his own home. On the other hand, he was curious about what the determined-looking girl could wish to say to him. Both he and James took their seats.

"I'm sure you can understand, after what happened, after I returned home it jarred with all the - the normality of the world. I had to learn more. And what I learnt was terrible. I want to be of use to you, to the Council, I want to join the witch-hunters."

Hunter sighed. To be honest, it wasn't uncommon for those rescued from the witches to feel in debt to the witch-hunters. And there was a perfect place for these untrained post-victims...

"Well, the Malleus Maleficarum Council always needs to employ people for its offices. There's lots of ways to help," Hunter replied. Yes, lots of ways to help, stuck in four walls organising counselling for victims, processing artifacts from raids, registering bound witches... More than a little bit dull.

Sophie seemed aware of that, and she shook her head. "No. I want to join the witch-hunters. I want to do something, Mr Astley."

Hunter grew uncomfortable at this, he did not enjoy recruiting witch-hunters. "It's not that simple, Miss Murphy, are you sure you won't consider an office position?"

It wasn't something to be taken lightly, everyone with the MMC put their lives on the line just by associating with witch-hunters. But to be a witch-hunter, to enter a world of darkness and fear, to never be off duty from revenge and persecution, to gamble with your life every day until a guaranteed early death. No, Hunter did not enjoy recruiting naïve people to join this hard life. But one glance at Sophie told him that she wouldn't be easily dissuaded.

"Miss Murphy, I understand how you feel, but the best witch-hunters are born, you can't just become one by choice. No, don't interrupt. My father was a witch-hunter, and his before him and so on, over the generations I have gained a certain... protection. A protection that you don't have."

Sophie sat quietly, then rounded on James. "And what about you? Are you a predestined witch hunter?"

James looked uncomfortably towards Hunter. "Ah, no. I'm like you. New to this. What's called a first generation. Even though I've been at this for five years now and I'm fully trained - or as much as any can claim t' be, I'm dependent on Hunter here for my safety, and I'm seen as nowt more than a lowly assistant t' MMC."

"Then I have made up my mind. I'll become a witch hunter, whether it is with your Council or not." Sophie replied quickly, a clear challenge in her voice. "It's up to you now, Mr Astley, are you going to help me?"

Hunter sat back, regarding the girl. She had guts enough, but he didn't like new people, besides the guilt, they couldn't handle things as well as he could. "James, a private word, please." He said quietly, then stood up, leading the way out into the corridor, aware of Sophie's eyes following them.

James closed the door behind him and shrugged. "I know what you're thinking, Hunter, but she's got the right attitude. Why don't we get in touch wi' MMC and give her a go. After all, we always need to build our numbers..."

Build our numbers. Or in other words replace those lost.

Hunter sighed, the decision would technically lie with the Council, but both he and James knew that his opinion would weigh heavily on the outcome. "Sure, let her throw her life away. Get in touch with the MMC, James. Suggest putting her with Brian Lloyd - he doesn't currently have an assistant."

James pulled his mobile out of his pocket and wandered down the empty corridor; while Hunter turned and re-entered the sitting room.

"James is talking to the Council now. Can I get you a drink while we wait?" Hunter asked as he closed the door gently behind him.

Sophie nodded, knowing she'd won her case. "Tea, please."

Hunter pressed the intercom and shortly asked Charles to bring up some tea. Sitting back down again he stared towards Sophie. She was bloody stubborn, maybe she'd be one of the few first generations to survive this career. "You'll be joining Brian Lloyd as an assistant-"

"Not you?" Sophie broke in.

Hunter frowned, not happy to be interrupted. "No." He replied abruptly. He didn't want the trouble of taking on an untrained assistant. "Mr Lloyd is a good man, he's been hunting for years and he'll teach you a lot. He's a fifth generation and can protect you while you learn, then you'll work under him."

There was a light knock on the door and Charles walked in, carrying a large tray. "Anything else sir?"

"No, thank you." Hunter replied, lightly dismissing him as he leaned forward to serve the tea. How very British; having a nice cup of tea whilst conversing about witches.

"You keep talking about generations, what do you mean?" Sophie asked, accepting her cup.

"Exactly what I say." Hunter replied, sipping at the hot drink. "People like you, and James, are referred to as first generations, because that's what you are. If you live long enough to have children and they continue witch hunting, they're second generations. Mr Lloyd is a fifth gen, meaning that his father, grandfather, great- and great-great-grandfather all worked for the MMC. Which means that he is highly regarded at the Council."

"And what are you, then?" Sophie asked quickly.

"I'm a seventh generation."

"So you're even more 'highly regarded'?"

Hunter paused, staring down into his hot tea. When he continued, it was more haltingly. "Yes. For two reasons. First, I mentioned protection - it turns out that when the parent fights witchcraft, the children gain a certain resistance to it. It's like evolution in fast forward. By the third generation, they can perceive magic being used, they can deflect minor curses. By the fifth generation, they are stronger, faster…"

Sophie waited, but it seemed Hunter intended to leave the sentence hanging. "And? What about when a family gets to seven generations? What about you?"

Hunter now avoided her gaze. "Obviously I'm even better equipped… You have to understand that we don't know much about the skills of sixth and seventh gens. There are so few of us. Which brings me onto my second point - there are hundreds, perhaps thousands of first gens. Only about half of these survive long enough to even have families. And those of us that become a well-known witch-hunting family become a target for all witches." He now looked up to gauge her reaction. "You didn't think this would be a nine to five, did you? So many families utterly destroyed by witches to prevent the next generation of hunters. And then you have to start from scratch."

"I am not naïve, Mr Astley, I can boast to be somewhat aware of the risk of it all." She sipped the hot tea, then gazed with that constant frosty defiance at Hunter. "Besides, your family seems to have survived these dangers - even prospered."

It was clear that she assessed Astley success with the luxurious, sprawling manor. Hunter smiled at her confidence, but was a little unnerved at how cold Sophie was. Oh well, at least she was strong, who knew, perhaps she'd be ok. "Ah, well, over the

25

generations we've learnt how best to protect ourselves. Astley Manor, for instance, has its own protection."

He paused and looked at her carefully, gauging the girl's potential, before suddenly deciding why not. "Come, I'd like to show you something."

Hunter led the way into the back of the house. He took out a key and unlocked a heavy door. It was dark inside the room, heavy curtains drawn across every window. Hunter clicked on a light and walked in.

"This is one of the best libraries in Britain - witch related libraries, of course." Hunter gestured to the rows of shelves, the room was stuffed with books, papers, files... "It's one of the perks of 200 years of Astley family witch hunting."

He moved over to a large glass case, looking down at it with a smile. "My personal favourite."

Sophie went over, peering curiously at the large yellowed sheets, bound with what looked like leather straps. Faded ink was shaped in medieval handwriting that looked familiar, assumedly Latin. "What does it say?"

"Malleus Maleficarum, maleficas ut earum hæresim, ut phramea potentissima conterens. Which roughly translates as 'The Hammer of Witches which destroyeth Witches and their heresy like a most powerful spear'." Hunter read out the first couple of lines, his fingers tracing above the words. "It's from the-"

"Malleus Maleficarum: 'The Hammer of Witches' or 'Witch-hunter's Handbook'. Published 1487. You have an original printing, impressive." Sophie suddenly recited.

Hunter looked at her in surprise.

"As I said, I've been doing my own research." Sophie added with an off-handed shrug. "You can find out about anything on Google."

"Yes, well." Hunter walked over to a bureau and picked up another book, relatively new compared to the rest. "This is something you won't see on the net. The Malleus Maleficarum - 37th Edition. The Handbook gets updated every thirty years or so. This was brought out four years ago." He handed her the book. It was small, only A5, but thick. And when she opened it and flicked through the pages, the text was small and dense.

"These are given to witch-hunters only." Hunter said, reclaiming his copy. "The Council will give you one when you are ready. I'm sure you'll find it as interesting as reading the Bible, but it's a sorry necessity to know it well. In the meantime, there is something I'd like to give you."

Hunter turned to a little dark door and another key was taken out. It was cold on the other side and as a pale light flickered on, Sophie followed down a set of stone steps. As she reached the bottom she shivered. It was a large stone room, which had originally been designed as a wine cellar.

Now it was like a private museum for the occult. One case displayed a score of knives and daggers, all remarkably designed. A long shelf held a bizarre collection of bottles - containing what Sophie dare not guess. Everywhere there was the glitter of silver bowls, the gleam of bronze bands.

"What is this stuff?" Sophie asked, still gazing about in amazement.

"Just stuff collected over the years. Things my family have confiscated from the witchkind. Some of it is quite useful." He pulled at the chain around his neck and lifted out a soldier's dog tags. "This, for example. We think it was originally used for protection during World War Two. It's served me very well when I've gone up against witches. It deflects all sorts of spells and attacks - it must've been a very strong witch that made it."

Sophie looked disgusted. "You horde dead witches' stuff? And then use it?"

"It's not as bad as it sounds. Well, ok, maybe it is. But we're not going to turn down extra protection. Anyway, it's safe. Dangerous stuff is disposed by the Council. Everything else is analysed, then returned to the witch-hunter. Most of us have an amulet of some sort."

Hunter turned to a cabinet and took out a silver necklace with a cloudy stone hanging from it. "Look, I'd like you to take this with you."

Sophie reached out and took it, then turned it over carefully in her hand. "I don't know what to say." She replied quietly, her eyes lowered.

Hunter shrugged. He wasn't one to throw gifts at relative strangers, especially not when the gift came from his own collection, but he felt incredibly guilty about setting Sophie up for a dangerous life.

"HUNTER!" James did insist on shouting in Hunter's house, even though Astley Manor was equipped with a state-of-the-art intercom system.

Hunter traipsed up the stairs again, followed closely by Sophie.

"Hey, it's sorted." James said quickly, "Sophie's gotta go straight to Brian Lloyd. He's his usual grumbling, unhappy self about it, but he's expectin' her."

"Right! That's great." Hunter turned to Sophie and shook her hand briefly, "Nice meeting you again, Miss Murphy. Brian will give you a good start, you'll learn a lot. James will give you directions and see you out."

And that was it; Hunter turned and left for the second time expecting not to have to see Sophie Murphy again.

Three

Despite his promise to keep his distance, to let the girl get on with her training, business carried Hunter to Brian Lloyd's door. James was visiting family up north, and Hunter decided to use the time to go see Brian. The fact that he could discretely check on Sophie's progress had of course never occurred to him.

As he strolled up the driveway, he looked up at the familiar house. It was detached and roomy, though nothing compared to Astley Manor. Still, Hunter had spent a lot of time here. After his father had died – or more correctly, been killed – Brian had stepped in. The MMC were desperate for the 7th gen Hunter to reach his full potential, preferably while keeping him tethered to the Council. So they had sent 5th gen Brian Lloyd, to continue his training.

There weren't many people that Hunter was scared of, but Brian was one of them. Tall, stocky, with close-shorn hair, he looked tough and was an unforgiving bastard. But he was good at what he did and in

Hunter's opinion, he was always right. So it was with some nerves that he knocked on Brian's front door.

"Don't stand there gawping, boy. You coming in or not?" Without waiting for an answer, Brian went back into the house.

Hunter sighed, things obviously hadn't changed. He stepped through into a large study where Sophie sat, deep in reading a musty old volume.

"Oi, be useful, put the kettle on." Brian barked at her.

Sophie shot Hunter a cold look and took herself out of the room.

"So, how are things going?" Hunter asked with a smile. He'd had some equally pleasant experiences of training with Brian. It was almost satisfying to see that the old man was treating his next trainee with the same courtesy.

"I don't like you throwing your weight with the Council, boy. Sending me a bloody girl. What use are girls?"

Hunter gave his old mentor a sideways glance. Ah yes, Brian was set in the old ways, and at 62 years old, he wasn't about to change.

"Brian-"

"Oh aye, I know all about your modern, pc equality crap. But if she wants to help the MMC, why didn't you stick her in an office - registering bound witches, or filing cases."

"Because no one wants to do that boring shit." Hunter replied, then grinned, "So I take it it's not going well?"

"Ah well, I wouldn't say that. She seems to be coping, picking it up well enough. Took her along to a raid, she kept her head, didn't even throw up at all the blood."

Hunter found himself gazing in the direction of the kitchen where there was the clatter of mugs. What do you know, maybe Sophie would make a witch-hunter after all, and he wouldn't have to feel guilty.

"Ugh, you do like to try me, George," Brian grumbled.

"Who's George?" Sophie appeared in the doorway, three mugs in hand.

"Ahm." Hunter shifted uncomfortably, trying to work out if he could get a cup of tea without giving an answer.

"You didn't think Hunter was his actual name, girl?" Brian guffawed, blowing everything. "George Astley the Seventh, that's him. Only he insists on adopting that daft moniker and have everyone call him it. Just egotistical, if you ask me."

Sophie turned to Hunter, her eyes glittering.

"Look, I'll have you know my friends started that nickname - and it had nothing to do with witches. Besides, do I look like a 'George'? Only my mother insists on calling me it - well, and you, Mr Lloyd."

They sat drinking tea and chatting about insignificant things for another half hour. With a meaningful look from Brian, Sophie picked up some books and excused herself.

"You didn't just come for a chit-chat?" Brian asked suspiciously.

"No," Hunter replied, then fell silent. There was something else that had been making him increasingly uneasy, especially after a recent event.

"A police contact got in touch recently. He had something he thought I might be interested in. A couple of months ago six teenage girls died in a suspected arson attack."

"And why should that concern us?" Brian asked, not sure where this was going.

"Well, it turns out they were all wiccans."

The two men sat in silence. Wiccans. Whereas witches were a whole different breed, wiccans were normal humans (normal in perspective) that treated 'magick' as a religion. They were generally harmless individuals, bored housewives and teens that wore too much black. They played with their candles and foretold wobbly futures through cards and the like and were a bit of a running joke amongst the witch-hunters. After all, who'd be scared of a cat after facing lions!

Eventually Brian shrugged. "Sometimes wiccans die. It could have been an accident; it could have been arson, but mundane normal people arson. If witches were involved, the MMC would have found the traces."

"There's more." Hunter sighed. "And I don't know what to make of it. Last week, we took on a small coven, four witches. Three were killed, one bound. But as soon as the binding was complete, she burst into tears, saying crazy things: that she didn't know what she was agreeing to. Then she committed suicide a day later. Something didn't feel right so I had James do a background check. Turns out she was a wiccan."

Ok. That was enough to get Brian's attention.

"But... wiccans cannot gain anything from witchcraft."

"I know," Hunter muttered.

"What proud witch would allow one to join them. They think wiccans are scum."

"I know."

"And the binding, a wiccan would have no powers to be bound from, so why would she agree to be bound?"

"I know."

"So... are they taking on wiccans as servants? Or using them to swell their ranks? It's unheard of."

"That's what I was thinking," Hunter agreed. It didn't seem to fit, but he was scrabbling to make sense of it.

Brian sat, idly scratching his chin as he stared into space. He was a living legend, one of the oldest, longest-running witch-hunters. He'd faced every threat out there and never backed down. If he couldn't find an answer, who could?

"Aye, leave this to me, boy. I'll look into it. Now, why don't you bugger off so I can get some work done."

Hunter smiled again and shook hands with his old mentor. Yes, time to leave, there were other sources he could get working too.

As he left he passed Sophie who was sitting in the front garden, a book on her lap. She looked up as he said goodbye and there was the briefest smile on her lips. "See you, George."

*****

His next stop was Oxford.

Possibly one of the most beautiful cities in England. The way it clung onto tradition, and the studious air that came from the abundance of intelligent young minds. Oh, the memories Hunter had of this place. The slightly dilapidated rooms at his old college, the great hall that awed all newcomers, the underground bar where he used to drink with James and Charlotte.

It had been in his first year of university that he received the news that his father had been killed. Hunter joined the witch-hunters then and there and he'd dragged his friends into his dangerous world. Now they all had their parts to play. James was a 1st gen witch-hunter and Charlotte, dear sweet Charlotte, was a very important member of the Council: she had easily switched from law student to liaison in the office of bound witches.

So who better to ask about bound witches. Hunter rolled up to her door early the next morning. But the person that answered wasn't the black-skinned beauty, it was a tall, lanky bloke with glasses.

"Ah, morning, Steve. Is Lottie in?"

Steve King, the gormless bugger that had married the most important woman in Hunter's life. Steve King, who now looked with intense dislike towards Hunter.

"Charlotte, you've got a visitor!" Steve called, and then stepped aside so Hunter could squeeze into the hall. "She's in the kitchen."

Hunter nodded humbly and went through the familiar house, Steve close behind him. Something about that guy always made Hunter feel like he'd done something wrong. But then, Hunter always did go out of his way to antagonise him.

"Ah, my favourite lady, just how I like to see her!" Hunter greeted with a fierce hug.

Charlotte gave him a sceptical look when he let go. She was sat at the breakfast table with a half-eaten bowl of cereal in front of her. Her unbrushed black hair was tied messily back and she was still in her dressing gown.

"I wanted to catch you before you went to work."

"I'm not working today Hunter. You could have phoned ahead." Charlotte glanced at the clock. "Oh, darling, you're going to be late." Her big brown eyes fell on her husband. "Go to work, we'll be fine."

"Yes, go to work, darling. I'll look after Lottie." Hunter added, enjoying the opportunity to wind him up.

Charlotte jumped up to see Steve out the front door, hitting Hunter as she passed him.

Ignoring the loving farewell that echoed up the corridor, Hunter helped himself to the fresh coffee.

"I wish you wouldn't do that," Charlotte said as she came back, "Every time you visit, he's in a mood for a week."

"Then you shouldn't have married such a grumpy sod. Why you settled for such a boring-"

"Quiet, kind, caring and RELIABLE." Charlotte cut in, repeating what she had said a hundred times before. "Why are you here, Hunter? Apart from driving my husband mad."

Hunter repeated everything he'd told Brian. Told her everything.

"And you want me to look if we have any similar cases, and check out the backgrounds of any unusual cases?"

God she caught on fast.

Charlotte regarded him carefully. "That's a lot of extra work, Hunter. Do you know how many cases my office has processed?"

Hunter sighed. "I know, and I hate to ask, but I have a weird feeling there's something bigger here."

"Ok. I'll do it, of course," Charlotte replied with a sorry smile. "I learnt long ago to trust your weird feelings."

"Thanks, Lottie." Hunter gazed at her with friendly affection. But then frowned. "Where's your bracelet? You know you shouldn't take it off."

He was speaking of Charlotte's amulet, a delicate gold bracelet with small rubies, a beautiful way to protect oneself.

Charlotte reached into her dressing gown pocket and pulled out the offending piece of jewellery, her fingers gently playing over the links and stones. "Steve doesn't like me wearing it too often, no matter how I explain it he still sees it purely as an expensive gift from you that he can't compete with. But don't worry, I always have it close by."

Hunter frowned at this news, disliking dear Steve even more. "What if it doesn't work like that, Charlotte? You shouldn't take the risk."

"I'm a full-grown woman, Mr Astley, it's my choice."

Ok, so Hunter felt like the petulant little boy whenever Charlotte got like this, but he couldn't help caring. "Ok, but please tell me Steve hasn't removed the protection over the house?"

"No, he sees that as a dividend of working at the MMC. If you don't believe me, you can go inspect it." Charlotte said, looking carefully at Hunter. "Can we talk about something else? How's James?"

"Reliably annoying," Hunter replied swiftly. "He's gone home for a few days, which means he will come back with that unbearable over-the-top accent again. He might as well wear a bloody badge saying 'I'm from Yorkshire'."

Charlotte laughed, she knew that Hunter was as fond of James as she was, but that didn't stop these two southerners enjoying the peculiarities of their friend from oop north.

"And how's - what's her name - Leanne? All going well?" Charlotte asked, unconvincingly 'forgetting' the name of Hunter's girlfriend.

"Leanne?" Hunter asked vaguely. "Oh, her. She got too clingy. It's Marie now, but it's not going anywhere. Then there's Natalie of course, the girl from my mother's tennis club."

Charlotte laughed at the ever-changing women in his life. "Lord, I can't keep track of you, Hunter. What are you trying to do, work your way through the alphabet before New Year? Will it be Olivia next, then Patrice? Aren't you ever just going to settle down?"

Hunter shrugged. "What can I say? The best girl in the world is already taken, so I'm just enjoying the rest."

There was an uncomfortable silence, and Hunter wondered if he'd tripped over that invisible line of conduct they kept for their friendship. They both knew that he had been in love with her since their days at University. Charlotte was beautiful and intelligent, she had been so caring and supportive when Hunter's father had died. She had also been immune to his charms.

Charlotte had never returned his love, and their relationship had been awkwardly platonic. Some days it was more awkward than others.

Hunter was uncomfortably aware that today was going to be one of those days. He glanced at his watch, anxious for an excuse to leave. "Look, Lottie, I should be going. I promise I'll ring before I come round next time!"

Four

Back to work again, no matter what else was happening, the fight against witchcraft was ongoing. During James' trip to Yorkshire, he had heard of incidents that the MMC were yet unaware of. People in a small village were living in fear for their sanity. So they had done their research and headed up. For the past few weeks, several prominent figures of the small community had been suffering from hallucinations. Constant terrifying visions of those they loved dying in gruesome manners. It all started when the village united to drive away a disturbing new resident, a middle-aged woman they suspected of carrying out sick, occult practices. And it all reached a peak when the post-office owner was found dead - verdict suicide.

It seemed like an obvious case of a witch taking revenge.

Hunter and James arrived at the village in the evening, the last of the summer sun giving it a warm, pleasant look. But the serene picture was ruined by the fact that from the moment they arrived, Hunter could taste the layers of magic and the violent, bitter tone of the spells.

James hefted their bags out of the car and slammed the boot. "So where is she?"

They had managed to work out that the witch must be staying close to the village, but nothing more specific. That's where a trained witch-hunter came in - they could sense the use, and source of magic; and Hunter just happened to be a finely-tuned 7th gen.

He closed his eyes, seeing and feeling the rhythm of the last cast spell. His eyes flew open. "Hope you brought your hiking boots." He said, turning to James with a rueful smile.

Unfortunately magic didn't follow roads, or dry paths, and the two men pushed their way through a field of corn, then a field of wet grass, avoiding cowpats in the darkening evening. The land became more untamed and a small cottage appeared in a hidden dip of the countryside.

"There. Definitely there." Hunter said, finally stopping.

James caught up, slightly out of breath. He dumped his bag and pulled out his kit: Kevlar jacket; long knife; short knife; gun; in the bag there was everything he could possibly need. He checked them over, repeatedly checking the gold ring on his right hand, even though he never removed the protective amulet.

Hunter was kitted out in similar fashion. He turned and nodded to James and they set off the short distance to the cottage in silence. Over the years they worked together perfectly and it seemed unnecessary for extraneous words.

Hunter went to the front door, then waited to give James chance to get round the back. He knew when James was in place - Hunter never challenged his senses, even he didn't know how being a 7th gen allowed him to do this. Then, gun in hand, he opened the old, rusty latch on the door. It made a slight creak as it opened and Hunter held his breath, but there was no response. He opened it further and slipped in, creeping towards a flickering light, carefully, carefully over the rough wooden floor.

Hunter stopped at a doorway, gently inching round so that he could see part of the room. There was movement and he snapped back, then looked again. A figure was moving about, preparing for her night's work. Candles were lit, random objects arranged on the floor - personal items such as brushes, photos, even clothing - all to help focus the magic upon her victims. Hunter knew from his research that the woman was nearly fifty, but she had the appearance of a thirty-year old. It wasn't uncommon for witches to keep a youthful appearance, they were vain and arrogant creatures.

Hunter dragged his eyes across the room, searching for further danger. Then to the only other door, where a slight shift of shadow showed James was ready. Hunter nodded and stepped into the room, gun raised. "Stop!"

The witch jumped with surprise, she span round to see that there were two of them. But then she smiled and shook her head. She raised her arms and the shadow and firelight leapt up and formed two massive snarling beasts which rushed at the men.

Hunter didn't flinch, didn't move, as the very solid four-legged beast leapt up with teeth bared... and continued to pass straight through him.

The witch hesitated, disconcerted that her powerful illusions failed to distract these men.

"By the Malleus Maleficarum, you will surrender your-"

"Witch-hunters." The witch snarled, stepping back, her eyes sparking dangerously. "In that case..."

She kicked over the candles and before Hunter could react the fire sped with unnatural speed and threw up a wall of flame. Hunter fired once into the flames, but heard the bullet hit the wall. The fire twisted into a huge serpent and darted at James. He didn't move fast enough and his sleeve singed and ignited and he allowed himself to be distracted. The witch sent a wave of power that knocked him off his feet.

"No!" Hunter leapt to his friend's side so that he could protect them both, firing off another round as he did so.

The whole room was on fire now, the air thickening with smoke. The witch stood in the very centre, a smile on her face. But then Hunter heard the smashing of a window and the image faded - the illusion buying its master time to escape.

Coughing, Hunter dragged James to his feet and the two of them stumbled through the heat and smoke to the door. Once outside they gulped down the clean air, James dropped to the ground again, but Hunter turned and ran.

Across the dark fields, Hunter's sharp eyes could see a fleeing figure. He stopped as he reached higher ground and raised his gun, took aim and fired. In the distance the figure jerked and fell.

Still coughing, Hunter jogged along to his quarry. The witch was gasping for breath and fighting the shock of having a bullet in her shoulder.

Hunter aimed the gun at her head, just in case she had the energy for another round.

"As I was saying, surrender yourself to my authority, to be bound and charged."

The witch spat at him, then screamed. "She will be my saviour."

Hunter heard James stagger up to them as he cocked the gun. It was his experience that this attitude led to immediate execution.

But the witch seemed to claw back her wild anger and gave a grimace. "Bind me, you cowardly bastards." She dropped her head back to the ground, submitting to her disgraceful fate.

"If you will, Mr Bennett." Hunter said, without moving the gun.

James knelt down and pulled out an amulet and piece of black ribbon. He took out his small knife and cut the witch's thumb, then pressed it to the amulet and wrapped the black ribbon about her wrist.

The witch grew tense and screeched as her powers drained out of her and into the amulet.

Hunter watched dispassionately. He preferred not to kill, and now she was harmless - well, she was no more dangerous than a human now. Her power would be filed at the MMC, then disposed of; and she would be carted off to prison. A job well done, with only a few minor burns to deal with.

Only... Hunter felt uneasy. This witch had proved to be powerful, yet instead of fighting to the death, she had quickly given up on pride and been bound. It was unusual enough to make him worry. He sighed, telling himself to stop being daft, they had won.

*****

The offices of the Oxford Branch of the MMC hardly stood out. There was very little to differentiate between them and the other boring buildings that neighboured it. James had offered to take the recent deposits of files and amulets, but Hunter had insisted on doing it. After that last witch, James was still burnt and concussed. It was rather funny really, Hunter noticed that whenever good old James got concussed his Yorkshire accent got so bad that you could hardly understand the poor bloke. Besides, Hunter wanted to drop in and see Charlotte.

He knocked on the door and went in. "Hey, I brought flowers."

He handed over the bunch of yellow roses and looked at Charlotte with concern. She was always beautiful, but there was a strain in her face and she emanated tiredness.

"I - I came to see if you'd found anything?" Hunter asked, jumping straight to the point.

"Oh Hunter, they're lovely," Charlotte replied, taking them and breathing in the fresh scent. But then she shook her head. "I haven't found anything. I'm sorry, but I haven't had the time. We've had more bound witches to process this month than... well, than ever. Executions are down and bindings have shot up." She frowned and gently stroked the petals of a flower.

"And we're short staffed. I don't know if you've heard, but Diane was killed, along with her family. She didn't turn up for work on Monday. They found her in the family home. Rick and little Josie, too."

Her eyes teared up, but she blinked them away. Everyone died, it was just a question of when.

"Oh, I didn't mean that the short-staffing was the worst thing. I meant... You know what I meant." Charlotte added, feeling worse the whole time.

"I'm sorry." Hunter murmured, feeling useless.

Charlotte closed her eyes and took a deep breath, settling her nerves. "We all know the dangers of working for the MMC, we know what we've signed up for. But sometimes you forget, just for a moment you forget and become attached to someone..."

Hunter watched Charlotte as she purposefully kept her eyes focused on the flowers, the timid nature of her voice only confirming how close to tears she was. Noting the redness around her eyes, Hunter wondered how many times she had cried for her colleague today.

Hunter felt a stab of guilt at how easily Charlotte acknowledged the danger they were all in. It wasn't a lie that, if she had never met him, she would be a valued lawyer somewhere. She never would have heard of witches and the Malleus Maleficarum Council.

Instead, she had joined the Oxford offices, and over the last few years Hunter had to watch her ascend to an important position. Hunter had wondered whether the quick ascension was only due to the Council realising what a bright star they had with Charlotte; or were they trying to mollify him.

"The funeral is on Friday, will you be there?" Charlotte asked, breaking his train of thought.

Hunter inwardly winced. He hated going to funerals, especially as there were so many in their line of work. They didn't help anyone, it was only one more occasion to feel awkward on.

Hunter could probably get away with not going, no one would dare openly say anything about his absence. But his absence would be noted, the famous Hunter Astley, unable to respect the passing of one of their own.

"I'll try." He finally answered, less than convincingly.

Charlotte's normally soft brown eyes were a little colder as she regarded him, a slight pout to her lips. "I'll text you and James the address."

Getting James involved was a threat. It was only one level lower than threatening to involve his mother.

Hunter grimaced, trying again. "We'll be there."

He stayed for a short while, then made his excuses and left. He could fight, kill if need be, but he couldn't face sorrow. Not even when one of his best friends needed his comfort.

Five

The call came just past midnight. Hunter set off immediately, picking up James on the way. They roared along the empty roads at 90mph, screw speed cameras and police, they had to get there.

Less than an hour later they screeched to a halt, both breathless with fear.

Hunter had been here only a month ago, but Brian's house was unrecognisable. The garden was all torn up and half of the house had fallen down, the rest was charred and still steaming.

Someone ran up as they saw them approach. The man was white-faced. "Hunter Astley? I'm Mathew Jones, 3rd gen." His voice cracked and he held out a shaky hand.

Hunter dragged his gaze away from the ruins. He shook hands, his actions robotic. "Brian?" He barely managed to ask.

The other man shook his head.

Hunter felt as though he had suffered a physical blow to his chest. Yes, it was a dangerous life and they were all living on borrowed time, but how could Brian be gone? He was the strong one, the survivor.

"Th-there was a girl." James finally spoke up, forcing his voice to steady. "An apprentice, Sophie."

Mr Jones got a hold of his emotions again. "Yes, she's alive. The ambulance took her away an hour ago. A few minor injuries, she was very lucky."

"What happened?" Hunter asked.

"We don't know for sure. Must've been a big coven, to do this much damage. Hopefully the apprentice can tell us more. I'll take you both to the hospital with me, if you want."

Hunter nodded. Yes, they should go to the hospital, see Sophie. But first, Hunter went up to the house. A couple of MMC staff came to warn him it wasn't safe (as if he needed telling), but let him go in, lending him a torch.

The blast must have been something fierce. Its source in the study, there was nothing left of this part of the house - walls, furniture, books - they were ash alike. Hunter stood amongst the rubble, the place throbbed with magic. Who the hell had this much power?

*****

The drive to the hospital was a blur. Soon they were marching down the half-lit corridors. Sophie was in a private room, propped up with pillows, waiting for them. Her arms were a mess of shallow cuts; a thick white pad covered her right shoulder where she'd needed stitches; the right side of her face was already bruising; and dust lightened her dark hair.

Even through the effect of pain-killers, and despite it being the early hours of the morning, she gazed clearly and calmly at her visitors. "I was wondering when you were going to turn up."

"Miss Murphy, we need you to tell us what happened tonight." Mr Jones asked, taking out a pad and pen.

"You should ask Brian, I won't be much help."

"Please Sophie," Hunter interrupted in a pained voice. "Just tell us what you can."

Sophie shrugged, then winced, her fingers tenderly feeling her injured shoulder. "Fine. It was late, near midnight. I was asleep up in my room when Brian came in, woke me up and told me to follow him quietly."

"Did he say why?" Mr Jones asked, scribbling away.

Sophie gave him a scathing look. "When you learn at the feet of Brian Lloyd, you do exactly what he says, you never question."

The witch-hunter looked slightly embarrassed, but Hunter, who knew this to be the blunt truth, quietly asked Sophie to continue.

"We went downstairs, to his weapons lock. He was in a hurry for us both to be kitted up. Then he just froze and said 'No time.' Then he said, 'I'm sorry.' And... and I saw pity in his eyes - he never... But anyway, next thing he locks me in that cupboard. There was no way out. A few minutes later, the place started to shake, then there was a massive blast. The world was turned upside down and I was knocked out. That's all I remember."

"Mhmn." Mr Jones continued to write. "Do you have any idea who was attacking?"

"No, I'm only a 1st gen. It was Brian that sensed the danger."

"And can you think of any recent cases, any events that might explain this huge attack?"

"Yes, no, I don't know." Sophie answered, getting riled up now. She grunted and put her hand to her aching head. "There were so many cases. We are witch-hunters, after all."

She looked up at Hunter, a clear demand in her eyes. "Where's Brian? No one will tell me how he's doing."

Hunter dropped her gaze. "He didn't make it."

"No." She sat in shock, her eyes darting to each of them as if willing them to deny it.

Mr Jones finally put away his notebook. "We're sorry for your loss, our loss. Once you've recovered, the MMC will make arrangements."

"I'm fine." Sophie replied curtly. "And I'm not staying in some hospital bed."

"She's coming with me." Hunter said quietly.

The other witch-hunter looked at him with surprise, knowing that he'd already taken on one 1st gen, and that Hunter Astley was a famously proud man.

"I can take on another apprentice. It's what Brian would have wanted."

It took until 11am to get Sophie discharged, and the doctors still weren't happy about it. Hunter drove back, James sitting in silent sorrow next to him, Sophie asleep on the back seat. Eventually they were pulling up on the gravel driveway at the front of Astley Manor. Hunter saw an unfamiliar car parked up, but was too tired to wonder.

Charles was at the door, waiting for them. "Good morning, sir. Mrs King arrived half an hour ago and insisted on waiting for you."

"Thank you, Charles." Hunter replied wearily. "Oh, and Charles, Miss Murphy is going to be staying with us. Will you prepare her a room?"

"Yes, sir."

Silence enveloped the three of them again, and they moved together into the sitting room.

"Hunter!" Charlotte jumped up from her seat as they entered. "I came as soon as I heard. It's - I can't believe it." Her eyes were red from tears already shed and they as threatened to spill again, Hunter pulled her into a fierce hug. This time he needed her, as much as she needed him.

"The grumpy old sod had a good running." Hunter muttered, making Charlotte gulp a laugh.

There was a clink of glass as James poured four drinks. He handed them out. "To Brian, loved and hated in equal measure."

Hunter raised his glass, "To Brian, the scariest bloke ever known."

Charlotte raised her glass. "To Brian, sexist, but brilliant."

The three old friends tapped their glasses together and drank, both cheered and saddened by their memories of him.

Sophie sat in quiet exclusion, in the corner. She sipped the warming alcohol, watching the group vaguely, her eyes still glazed with shock.

"Thanks for coming today." Hunter said to

Charlotte, later in the afternoon.

"I was planning to come, anyway. Oh, I almost forgot why." She said suddenly, turning to her handbag and pulling out a white envelope. "Brian and I were in contact a lot lately. Both of us were trying to solve your wiccan problem. He gave me this yesterday, before -" Charlotte broke off, then regained her composure. "He wanted me to pass it on to you."

Hunter frowned, taking the thick, unmarked envelope. He tore it open and pulled out the contents. A letter. The handwriting was ever so familiar.

> George,
>
> With luck, Charlotte King has given you this. I had to get this message to you without drawing further attention to myself. I'm in danger, and I no longer have the strength to fight it. All the same, I will never forgive myself for passing this onto you. But I don't know who else to trust.
>
> Things are worse than you thought. I can't go into detail in this letter. Charlotte has a key for you, it's for a locker, I've enclosed the address. In the locker is my research concerning your wiccan, and my own work I started last year.
>
> Hopefully I'll still be on hand to help you with this. But I had to write. Just in case.
>
> Yours,

Brian Lloyd
Beware the shadows

Hunter's hand shook as he passed the letter to the others. In the envelope was a slip of paper, just as he said. Charlotte silently slid him a small key.

"My God, it sounds as though he knew he was going to-" James muttered as he read it.

"Beware the shadows?" Charlotte repeated fearfully. "You don't think he means...?"

Hunter shook his head, in his hand he gripped the key so tightly it dug into his palm. "We'll know soon enough." Yes, he would go, find out what his mentor was being so secretive about. There was a new threat on the horizon, they could be sure of that at least.

But a wave of fatigue from the long day and its sorrows washed over him. There was nothing they could do until tomorrow.

"Tomorrow. Tomorrow."

Six

It was a long drive to Cumbria the next day. The fact that Brian had taken the precaution of hiding his research across the country, in such a random place, added to Hunter's fear of the enormity of what they might find.

Hunter would have gone alone, but James insisted on accompanying him, because how could he help if he wasn't there. Sophie, with some embarrassment, asked to come because she dare not be alone yet. Charlotte couldn't take such a trip - Hunter discovered with some dismay that she was suffering with morning sickness.

So Hunter and James sat in the front, arguing over whether to listen to Grimshaw or Evans, and Sophie sat in the back, reading quietly.

"So, you gonna to tell us where we're going?" James eventually asked.

"Carlisle." Hunter replied shortly.

"Carlisle? Christ, we'll be driving all day!" James twisted in his seat to look back at Sophie, "Hey, Soph,

55

did you know about Carlisle, I mean, did Brian say owt?"

Sophie glanced up from her book, frowning at the shortening of her name. "No. He never mentioned where he was going. He just used to disappear for a couple of days every fortnight. I just assumed he had a woman somewhere."

The two men shuddered at the thought of old Brian with a woman. And all settled in for a long drive.

*****

It was mid-afternoon by the time they got there. Hunter pulled up outside a plain building. "Keep the car running," He said to James. "I'll be back in a minute. Hopefully."

They waited in silence. James started to drum his fingertips on the wheel as he gazed out of the window avidly, as though expecting a witch to leap on them right there.

Sophie gritted her teeth against the annoying sound. "Can you stop that?"

"Sorry," James replied sheepishly. "Nervous."

Hunter wasn't long; he soon stepped out of the building with a large sports bag, which he dumped in the car boot before jumping back into the driver's seat and driving off without a word.

"You can't tell me we're going to drive all the way home before looking at what's in there?" Sophie asked sceptically.

Hunter grinned in the rear-view mirror. "You think we can wait that long?"

They drove until they were out of the town and kept going until they found a roadside picnic area. The place was empty, and it was quiet, except from the steady traffic that roared by, passengers ignorant of everything outside the car.

The three of them sat around a worn wooden bench, with the bag in front of them. Hunter glanced at the other two - this was it. He slowly unzipped the bag. Inside there were stacks of papers, some cardboard files and such. The three of them craned forward, then gingerly picked through it all.

"Well, here's some information on a period of intense persecution of wiccans by witches. It doesn't give dates on this sheet though." Hunter peered into the bag. "There should be the rest of it in there..."

"Hm, this file has records of witches and wiccans from - wow, the 1940s," Sophie voiced.

"Well, this might be important, but I'll be damned if I can read it," James said, as he leafed through some old papers with scrawled handwriting.

They continued to look through the work for another half-hour, it seemed as though Brian had a unique way of ordering things. They made no immediate discovery to how it was all linked, nor to why it was so important to Brian. It was quite the anti-climax.

James was the first to admit defeat. He pushed the papers back into the bag. "Look, we aint gonna solve this in the next five minutes, and I feel uncomfy havin' these out in the open."

"Home we go then" Hunter suggested, not relishing another five hour drive.

"Actually," Sophie interrupted. "My mum doesn't live far away, over in the Lake District. I was going to ask if you could drop me off - I haven't seen her since I joined Brian. But I'm sure she'd put us all up for the night, and we can drive down tomorrow."

"I vote yes," James immediately piped up.

"Be careful, Sophie, that was you almost being nice to us," Hunter teased. "But yes, why not. And we get to meet your mother!"

*****

The countryside was beautiful, wild hills and deep valleys, the road twisted and rose and fell to make its way through nature. Often a wide expanse of water lay off to one side or the other, a few boats still out on the lakes on a fine evening. With Sophie's directions they came to the village of Keswick and were soon pulling up outside her mother's house. It was an old cottage on the outskirts of the village and the whole atmosphere of the place was one of rough country warmth.

Hunter lugged the big bag with him as he and James followed Sophie up to the front door.

"Mum!" Sophie called out as she opened the door.

The figure of Mrs Murphy quickly came to meet them, the poor woman getting a shock at the state of her daughter; she reached out, tenderly touching the darkly-bruised face, her eyes taking in the fresh cuts on Sophie's bare arms. "Oh my darling, my Sophie."

Mrs Murphy was just as tall as her daughter, just as graceful in figure. It was easy to see where Sophie got her looks from. Although when Mrs Murphy finally turned to her visitors, it was with a softer expression than her daughter had ever managed.

"Mum, this is Hunter and James, my colleagues," Sophie introduced.

58

All softness that Hunter perceived was suddenly revoked when Mrs Murphy worked out that these were the evil witch-hunters that had led her daughter astray.

"Mum, these were the ones that saved my life, when I was in Italy." Sophie stressed each word, warning her dear mother to behave herself.

"It's nice to meet you, Mrs Murphy," Hunter said, extending his hand.

"Please, call me Bev," She replied with a polite smile, still undecided on whether to like these two young men. "I'm afraid all I can offer our guests is the fold-out settee in the conservatory. I'll let you put your bags - er, bag down."

She showed them through the small cottage to the make-shift guest room. As oldy-worldy and traditional as the cottage had looked from the outside, the interior was all cool, modern lines and light colours. Hunter and James politely dawdled in the warm conservatory, giving Sophie time with her mum. But eventually they joined them back in the small living room.

The two women were sitting together on the settee, heads close as they talked, and Bev didn't look happy. "You shouldn't be travelling in your condition, only out of hospital. Oh that you ended up in hospital!"

"Mum! It was my choice to do this, and I don't regret any of it. I've already explained how important it is." Sophie stressed, holding her mother's gaze until the older woman dropped her eyes.

"Why you have to choose such danger, I don't know. You could have left it to others." Bev said bitterly. She then looked up, noticing the two men hovering by the door. She blushed at being overheard.

"Well, I suppose none of you will have eaten. You'll have to make do with my cooking."

Before anyone could say anything, or offer to help, Bev took herself off to the kitchen.

"Don't pay her any attention," Sophie said harshly. "She doesn't blame you guys - or at least, she shouldn't. She doesn't agree with my decision to join the MMC, as you probably heard."

"She's got a right to be worried," James replied with a shrug.

Sophie sighed, twisting to look towards the kitchen, clearly annoyed with her mother.

"Come on, she's not that bad for a mum, she cares for you, that's all," James continued. "Just wait til you meet Hunter's!"

Hunter gave him a scathing look. "Nobody wants to hear about her. So was this where you grew up?"

"Yes."

"What? That's it? No childhood stories you want to share?"

Sophie looked at both of them questioningly. "No. What's to tell? I grew up, then left to work in the city. If you're wanting tales of mad, rebellious youth, I've got to disappoint you."

*****

An hour later, Bev came to tell them dinner was ready, and they followed her to the delicious smells of toad-in-the-hole.

"Brilliant." James grinned as he sat down, loving everything that remotely resembled Yorkshire Pudding.

Hunter sat down, noticing that Bev looked calmer now. It must have been the shock of seeing her

60

daughter injured. Now the older woman was bordering on friendly.

Over dinner, they all started to chat about small things - Mrs Murphy quizzing the two men over every detail she could think of; how they'd gotten into witch-hunting? Had they gone to university? Oh, Oxford, what did they study?

She smiled down at her more reserved daughter. "I can see why you were so interested in witch-hunting, Sophie, not all professional is it? Yes, you'll have to excuse my daughter, she does have a romantic side to her."

Hunter had to stop himself choking on his food, and he looked up, seeing that James shared the joke. Sophie, romantic? Sure, if she wasn't such a frozen bitch.

Sophie frowned at her teasing mother's insinuations. "Behave yourself, mother, or I'll lock you in the pantry again."

The rest of the evening passed agreeably enough, but as they were all about to retire, Bev held Hunter back.

"Look, I know you mean well, and I'm sure you're a nice boy, but I don't want you to get involved with my daughter."

Hunter was surprised at the cold look Bev gave him, "Look, Mrs Murphy-"

But Bev stopped him. "You should be going to bed, Mr Astley. I'm assuming that you'll want to set off early tomorrow."

Then she left him. Ugh, bloody parents. With the exception of his own mother, it seemed they were all over-protective.

Hunter went into the conservatory, where the settee had been pulled out into a double bed, James already sitting in it - fully clothed, thank goodness.

"Hey, there's always the floor." James laughed in response to Hunter's grimacing expression.

"No, I just hope you don't snore tonight. Budge over."

The light was clicked off and the two mates lay there, both awake.

"So… Sophie's mum seems ok, she really warmed up after a while. I thought she was gonna kick us out when she heard we were witch-hunters."

"Yeah," Hunter grunted noncommittally. Mrs Murphy had changed from hostile to friendly in the blink of an eye, finishing things off with that motherly warning. Hunter decided that he preferred Sophie's frosty personality – at least he knew where he stood with her.

"I was thinking, about Sophie." James continued, not taking the hint. "I mean, she's a bonny lass. What do y'think, I got a chance? Or do you think the timing's inappropriate, you know with Brian and all."

Hunter sat bolt upright. "Look, just because we're sharing a bed, doesn't make this a girly sleepover."

"Ah, sorry mate."

Hunter lay down again. What did he think? That he was likelier to get any girl over James, harsh but true. But then he wasn't interested in Sophie; cold, beautiful

Sophie. At least, he wasn't interested in that way. "Just do me a favour, James. Wait until we all get home."

Seven

Home. Astley Manor was, and always had been a stuffy place to live. Growing up, Hunter associated the place with unspoken unhappiness, even before he knew about witches and his parents' unhappy marriage.

But now, it was full of life for the first time in a long while. Sophie seemed to be settling in, and it was just common sense for James to stay too - there was plenty of room after all. And since Brian's death, not a day went by without witch-hunters, Council staff, and especially Charlotte, coming for one reason or another.

Hunter enjoyed the company. His mother did not.

Hunter found it quite funny, how it riled the stuck-up old bag. Yes, of course he loved her, or at least he felt dutiful as her son, but Hunter definitely took after his father.

Sophie had a bit of a shock when meeting Mrs Astley. The first time they saw each other was in the breakfast room the morning after they came back from the Lake District. Sophie came down, still in her dressing gown and slippers, her unbrushed hair scraped back into a hair band.

Mrs Astley, in stark comparison was already dressed (in miserable black) and had done her hair and make-up before even daring to set foot outside her room. She was a very petite woman in her early fifties, but looked older, with narrow, pinched features. Her hair, which had once shone a silvery blonde, was now pale, washed of all colour and pulled into a harsh bun.

Her cold eyes fell on Sophie, immediately analytical. "Oh no, George. She won't do at all. Too fat and too common."

Sophie was taken aback by the sudden harshness from the little elegant woman. She looked about the room and saw Hunter sitting rather sheepishly in the corner, reading a newspaper.

"Mother, Sophie and I aren't… she's a witch-hunter. In training, anyway."

"I don't know, George. Taking in all these waifs and strays - it's just not nice." Mrs Astley said to her son, as though Sophie wasn't there. "Filling the Manor with all sorts. Well, I suppose your late father would have approved." Disgust entered her thin voice. "Cursed be the day I met him."

"Mother." A sharp warning came from Hunter, who immediately folded up his paper and stood up. He didn't look particularly angry, more resigned to suffering her bad manners.

"Come on, Sophie, I'll get you some breakfast," Hunter invited.

"That is what Charles is for!" The sharp voice followed as they left the room.

"Sorry about her. I think she enjoys adding more misery to the world." It was harsh, but true. Mrs Astley seemed to have no purpose in life except to criticise everyone else.

Later, once Sophie was dressed (although not to Mrs Astley's standards), Hunter offered to give her the guided tour of Astley Manor. It was a beautiful old house and they walked through the array of rooms, all stuffed with priceless antiques and portraits, Hunter keeping a running commentary as they went.

"There's George Astley II. He was the first to own the Manor," Hunter informed, pointing to a portrait cracking with age, where a suitably regal looking fellow posed in gold clothes and a white permed wig.

"I see the resemblance," Sophie retorted, almost making a joke. "Where's your portrait?"

"Ah, I don't have one. I keep putting it off," Hunter confessed. Then invited her to continue the tour. They occasionally passed more portraits of increasingly recent George Astleys, the clothes changing drastically, but the faces all familiar.

They stopped at the newest portrait, painted in the 1970s when the man in the picture was the same age as Hunter now. Hunter looked up with a sad recognition.

"And this is my father, known to one and all as Young."

Sophie gave him a questioning look that made him smile, and he hastened to explain. "It gets confusing when you're all called George Astley. I get called Hunter because that's the nickname my friends gave me. My father was always called Young, because his

66

father was known as Old George. See, it all makes perfect sense."

"Yeah, sure," Sophie replied, unconvinced. But she continued to look up at the portrait. "He looks nice."

"He was. He was lively, always off having adventures and coming back with wild stories. He'd make friends with everyone he met. And of course he was a great witch-hunter."

"You sound like you miss him," Sophie added in her usual cold manner. Hunter almost felt offended.

"Come on, I'll show you the gardens."

Outside the sun was shining, it was another lovely summer morning and there was the lazy buzz of bees over the well-kept flowers. Hunter and Sophie walked side by side through the perfect flowerbeds and sculpted hedges.

"When did he die?" Sophie asked, not being distracted from the topic of Hunter's father.

"Just over five years ago." Hunter replied. It wasn't that he was ashamed, or emotional talking about Young, he just never did. "I was in my first year at Oxford when the news came. The witches finally caught up with him."

"I'm sorry," Sophie said perfunctorily.

Hunter shrugged, "It happens, inevitably. But hey, how do you like the gardens? My mother keeps them. Not that she's particularly green-fingered, but she does enjoy ordering the gardeners about, telling them how to do their job and so on."

Mrs Astley was a character for endless jokes and ridicule. The old bag was probably aware that she wasn't popular with people in general, but that didn't stop her.

"Your mother, she's..." Sophie paused, wondering how best to phrase it. "Your parents were very different, weren't they?"

"Oh yes!" Hunter replied with a laugh. "They were too different, absolutely hated each other, they were always arguing when I was young. Oh, the memories."

"But they got married?"

"Yes. I suppose they were in love at one point. My father was the rich, handsome witch-hunter that saved a beautiful young lady from being sacrificed." Hunter gave the summary of their meeting. "As you heard, my mother often expresses the wish that she had been left to be killed. I can honestly say that I had an interesting childhood, growing up in that atmosphere."

On that sorry note, they continued quietly about the gardens, allowing Sophie to view the Manor from every angle. And it was a beautiful and suitably impressive place. There was just one small, niggling little detail.

"How on earth do you have a place like this and stay safe?" Sophie asked, her eyes fixed on the building. "You said that famous families were a target for witches. Surely this Manor is a beacon to them."

Hunter looked at her, it was a smart question, and he was surprised that she remembered what he had said so long ago. "You've still got the necklace I gave you?"

Sophie's hand went to her neck. "Yes."

"And I told you that was personal protection. Well, the Manor is filled with layers of enchantments and protective amulets and wards built into the very walls and doorways. No witch is ever going to find this place, and even if they did they couldn't do anything."

"What about sharing this protection?" she asked sharply. "I think Brian could have benefited from it."

Hunter was shocked to see fire and anger in her expression. Did she blame him for Brian's death? How could she? "Sophie-"

She cut him off by walking away. But Hunter wasn't about to let her go with this misconception. He caught up with her, grabbing an uninjured section of her arm and ignoring her fierce glare.

"Look, all witch-hunters and Council staff have the best protection the MMC can provide. But sometimes a strong group of witches can overcome these measures. We all do the best we can. And yes, I thought Brian was safe. Obviously not. I will not feel guilty about the safety of the Manor - as for sharing, I couldn't even if I wanted to because I don't understand half of it."

"Finished?" Sophie asked curtly.

Hunter felt the heat from his rant fading quickly. "Yes." He replied quietly, releasing her arm and watching Sophie walk away. He stayed where he was. He couldn't be blamed for Brian's death, no more than he could be blamed for any fallen witch-hunter, unless he invited them all to live in his Manor.

He kicked the nearest plant, sending petals flying. Now he would feel guilty about that - his mother would probably blame this imperfection on the gardeners when she saw it.

Oh well. He went back inside, making straight for his library. But Hunter stopped by the door, it was open and together at the desk, Sophie and James sat conspiratorially close.

Did Hunter feel jealous, looking at that cosy little scene? No, it must be something else. Whatever it was, Hunter felt no compulsion to join them just now. Let James have time with Sophie, so he might learn how unforgiving she was.

Eight

Every once in a while they all suffered to sit through the charade of a civilised dinner. Hunter, as master of the house, sat at the head of the table; his mother, styling herself as Astley Manor's own dowager empress, sat opposite him at the far end of the slightly too long table. This suited Hunter to have his mother seated as far away as possible, and he often employed the use of candelabras or a vase to block her from view completely.

James and Sophie submitted to sitting wherever Mrs Astley decided in her elaborate ideas of a perfect seating plan, even for such a small party. After all, it was easier to go along with something so harmless to keep the stubborn bag appeased.

Unfortunately, today Mrs Astley was in a talkative mood, and she raised her sharp voice so that her unimportant comments could be heard clearly down the table.

"And at least Mrs Harsmith has daughters to keep her company now Mr Harsmith is gone. All Mr Astley deigned to give me was an adventurous, cad of a son. Although I don't doubt you have half-sisters across the whole of England, George. But why I couldn't have had a daughter instead. You must get married, George, so that I might have a daughter-in-law, preferably before I die of old age."

Hunter smirked and nearly choked on his soup. In the corner of his eye he could see the slight shake of James' shoulders, as he too found Mrs Astley amusing. The newcomer, Sophie, seemed frozen in her seat, eyes wide at the open berating at the dinner table.

"Don't slurp your soup, George. Oh, you are too much like your father - I had hoped that a man from such an old family would have been well-mannered - well-moneyed was more like it. Young was as disgustingly common and ill-behaved as those football louts that always appear on the news."

"No he wasn't mother," Hunter corrected, protective of the memory of his father.

"Don't be so sure. Going to scruffy pubs, coming back drunken on cheap beer, swearing." Mrs Astley broke off, aghast at the mere thought of it. "Oh, I wish the witch had killed me, death would have been preferable to a torturous lifetime with Young."

"Mother, please remember that we have guests." Hunter said, before she could get too depressive.

Mrs Astley looked up, as though surprised to see James and Sophie there, she frowned at her son's assumption.

"Guests? I see no guests. I see two of your witch-hunter underlings that have the cheek to live off our kindness. That you live beside your staff as equals, George! It is most unbecoming."

"They are my friends, and as I am master of this house they shall remain here as my guests for as long as they like." Hunter replied with bite.

"Friends? Oh, you keep such bad company. When I think back to the boys from school - why don't you keep in touch, invite them to stay? Better them than these two. The girl is pretty, I admit, but I doubt she has a drop of good blood in her body. As for the young man, that hideous voice resonates through the house, the indecipherable accent - and what's more he's proud of it!"

Hunter sat back in his chair, a clenched fist by his mouth and his body near shaking. He was torn between anger and amusement, his mother was irritating and offensive, but the old girl was bloody entertaining.

*****

"Bring Sophie out into the yard, James." Hunter ordered, shrugging a light jacket on.

Hunter made his way into the courtyard at the rear of the house, the smooth square open on one side to the fields beyond where high grass browned in the weak summer sun. He gently dropped the bag he was carrying and knelt down to open it, sorting through the necessary tools of training it contained.

Hunter rose at the sound of footsteps behind him as James and Sophie came obediently to meet him. It had been five days since the attack at Brian's house and although misleadingly upbeat, Sophie still showed the physical marks of the tragedy, her skin coloured with bruises and her shoulder thickly padded with bandages. But hurt or not, Hunter wanted to waste no time - he'd already waited these five days with impatience.

"All right, Sophie, I need to know what Brian managed to teach you about attack and defence." Hunter said seriously. He held out a small dull object which Sophie took gingerly.

"It may seem brutal, but guns are our main weapons," Hunter said in response to her reaction, then bit his tongue, fearing to sound too apologetic. There was nothing to be sorry about, violent witches had to be killed, and was there a more efficient method?

"I want an idea of your aim. Now," Hunter pointed out across the field, about 100 yards away a wooden board stood, targets painted in fading colours. "Aim and fire."

Sophie glanced at both men with a moment's uncertainty, then took a deep breath and did as she was bid. The gun went off with a mighty crack that reverberated about the courtyard and made Sophie jump.

Hunter ignored her, his sharp eyes watching the bullet miss the entire board. "Don't rush. Later, when a witch is charging you down with spells blazing - that is when you are permitted to rush. But here and now I want accuracy, not speed. Try again."

Sophie scowled at Hunter's little criticizing speech, but said nothing in return. She raised the gun again, and altered her aim, taking her time, focusing on a spot slightly lower, as Brian had taught her.

She fired again. This time there was a satisfying 'thuck' as the bullet embedded itself in the board, just off the target.

"Better. Again." Hunter simply said.

Sophie repeated the process, making her corrections to aim. The third bullet hit the target dead centre. She almost smiled and tilted her head in an arrogant pose. Hunter still ignored her.

"Perfect," he commented. "Again."

Sophie frowned but continued, firing until the chamber was empty and her ears were ringing.

"Not too bad, I suppose," Hunter admitted. "But I want you to practise daily. I'm sure James can give you extra tuition if you find you need it."

Hunter's comment made James redden and Sophie scowl, but he just smiled in a knowing manner.

"Right, James help Sophie into a vest," Hunter said, pulling the black stab jacket out of the bag and tossing it to James while he retrieved two tapered poles.

James caught it clumsily, hesitating. "You're - you're gonna make her fight?"

"How else am I to assess her abilities?"

James opened his mouth to say something, but thought better of it. He reluctantly took the vest and held it up for Sophie to shrug into, then fitted it snugly about her slim figure.

Sophie ignored James' lingering hands on her waist and took one of the tapered poles from Hunter, it was about a foot long and made of smooth, solid wood. She looked up at Hunter, her expression giving nothing away.

"Now, until you learn to handle yourself properly, it's safer using these. If you manage to improve, we'll move onto real knives," Hunter instructed. "So, take first position as Brian taught you, and attack me as though I were a witch."

Sophie remained still. "You're not going to put on a vest?"

"You won't hit me," Hunter replied condescendingly. "First position, if you please Miss Murphy."

Sophie bit her tongue and prepared, pole raised, her balance evenly placed over both feet and flexible.

"And attack," Hunter ordered.

Sophie lunged forward, driving the tapered point of the pole at Hunter's chest. Faster than she could follow, her pole was knocked aside with a stinging crack and Hunter was off to a side, his pole an inch from her ribs. Sophie caught her breath and stared at him in amazement.

"How...?"

"Seventh generation," Hunter replied shortly. "You were too slow, even for a first gen. Try again. First position, and attack."

Sophie threw herself into the movement with all her strength, but again her pole was knocked aside and Hunter's was hovering at her neck. This time he was frowning.

"Too erratic. You need to be fast, accurate, or you're dead." Hunter wiped his face with his hand, as though trying to rub a growing headache out of his forehead. "Great. Right, back to basics."

They spent the next hour going through every position and motion, repeating again and again, Hunter correcting every minor flaw, accepting nothing but perfection. Sometimes he pulled James in to model and practise a succession of moves.

Eventually Hunter was happy enough to allow practise bouts again. He stood across from Sophie, whose face was already paling with the hint of exhaustion. They came to, this time Sophie moved correctly and there was the attack, parry, attack, parry, with the clacking rhythm of a violent dance. But Sophie slipped up and Hunter got past her guard, barely stopping his pole from jabbing her hip.

"Again." He demanded.

They came to again and again, each time Sophie fighting more desperately, each time she slipped up Hunter's patience shortened and he began to tap her harder with the pole, until he snapped at her incompetence and hit her harder than he meant to.

Sophie shouted in pain and shock and Hunter dropped his pole, eyes wide in self-disgust, but no apology reached his lips.

"Hunter!" James stepped in, angry with his friend, protective of Sophie. "Come on, that's enough for today, she's knackered. You 'ad no right to hit her, she's still hurt."

"She's got to learn." Hunter replied quietly, stooping to collect his pole from the ground.

"That's no reason -"

"James! I don't need your pity nor protection," Sophie interrupted sharply. She glanced at Hunter. "Again."

Hunter looked guiltily into that usually pale face that was now flushed with pain and exertion. "Look Sophie, if you're hurt, maybe…"

"I'm not in pain, I'm…" Sophie sighed, her annoyance clear and moved into first position, she spoke in a low and determined voice. "Again."

Hunter reluctantly raised his pole and nodded. Again there was the crack of wood on wood as they parried and pushed and circled. An aura of determination emanated from Sophie. She gave a great shout of rage as she attacked and her pole passed through Hunter's block and grazed his elbow.

Hunter stepped back and looked at her in surprise. He hadn't been holding back - not much anyway - it was a rare person that could land even the slightest blow on him.

"That's better," he conceded. "Let's call it a day. James can be your practise partner for the rest of the week."

Sophie pushed back her dark hair, damp with sweat, still breathing heavily she flashed a victorious smile at James who couldn't take his eyes off her.

*****

The James and Sophie "episode" didn't last very long.

At first, James had restrained himself to being a helpful, but constant presence for Sophie: Always there to offer company, or just a cup of tea; always on hand to help with a difficult translation of foreign text, or unravelling Brian's messy handwriting.

Hunter watched his friend's progress with a detached interest. After all these years, had impulsive, coarse James finally learnt tact and charm? It was almost disappointing to see things go so smoothly between him and Sophie. The sensible part of Hunter thought that it would be best for James and Sophie to have a mature relationship that wouldn't compromise their work. Unfortunately, this sensible part was dwarfed by a hope that Sophie would get out her claws as soon as James made his move, regardless of a happy working environment. For entertainment purposes only, of course, Hunter had no other reason to not see his two companions together.

The results of James efforts came to fruition one very normal afternoon, a fortnight after Sophie had joined them in Astley Manor. Hunter had just had a long, detailed conversation on the phone with someone at the MMC. They'd wanted to know (in an indifferent manner) how Miss Murphy was settling in, whether she'd remembered anything more from the night Brian had died. Hunter had dutifully filled them in on her state of recovery and that they had taken her to visit her mother - neatly failing to mention Brian's parting gift.

The droning voice on the other end of the phone had given Hunter a headache. Oh well, nothing cured a headache like staring at a load of musty old books!

As Hunter walked down the corridor, Sophie exited the library in a hurry, slamming the door behind her, then scowling and marching purposefully in his direction.

"Did you put him up to it?" She demanded, eyes blazing.

"Did I - what?" Hunter stuttered, taken aback.

"James, did you encourage him to…" Sophie broke off, too furious for words. "And I was foolish enough to think he was being kind for kindness sake. Can no one in this bloody world see me as a witch-hunter, rather than a girl that needs to be partnered off?!"

Her question was rhetorical and she was already storming off by the time she'd finished ranting. Hunter smiled grimly as he heard the front door clanged shut as Sophie left the Manor. He had a notion why Sophie was so mad.

Curious as to the particulars, Hunter resumed his short walk to the library. True to form James had his head in a book - at least he looked busy.

"James?" Hunter asked mildly. "What have you done?"

"Nuthin'," He grunted in reply.

"Of course. So Sophie is raging for no reason."

James looked up, his face was flushed red with either embarrassment or anger, Hunter couldn't tell which.

"It were nuthin'. I just asked Sophie out for a drink an' she said no." James replied with an overly nonchalant shrug.

Hunter watched him sceptically. "And what else did you say to upset her so badly?"

"Nuthin'." James repeated.

"Very well, if you've said nothing to offend Sophie, I'll have a word with her, get her to apologise for her temper." Hunter replied innocently.

"I-I may've been a bit rude." James finally confessed. "I mean, she had no reason to be so abrupt, not when I'd been so nice to her an' everything. So I might've called 'er a tease - a vicious tease. And I might've said she were shallow an' arrogant."

Hunter shook his head, he wasn't sure whether he found it all too funny, or too upsetting. "You'll have to say sorry."

"Hey, she gave as good as she got," James argued.

James seemed to miss the point about being a charming gentleman, it wasn't the looks and confidence that was valuable, it was being the first to apologise, and the last to say an unkind word.

"Why did you get so wound up?" Hunter asked, thinking that this was bad even for James.

James shrugged and looked away. "Dunno. There's just something about her. I liked her, and after all that effort she didn't feel the same way. Said she weren't interested in no-one. But I figure she's lying, probably just waiting for a better offer than common ol' me."

Hunter tried to ignore the bitter, hurt tone in his best friend's voice. It was hard enough hearing this unusually open confession. But James would get over it, Hunter selfishly hoped that it wouldn't affect his work.

The final insinuation made Hunter frown, it seemed like everyone expected him to swoop down on the beautiful Sophie.

"Well, I can promise you that the ice bitch isn't going to get a better offer in this house," Hunter replied with slightly forced humour.

James smiled and relaxed, made a little happier with Hunter's promise.

*****

It had been a long day. Hunter was still wearing his suit from the memorial service held for Brian Lloyd. It had been a suitably miserable day as the black-clad crowd stood about a plinth, erected to commemorate the greatest witch-hunters.

Witch-hunters had come from all over Britain, and there were even those from foreign MMCs. Hunter had always known that Brian Lloyd was special, but his personal closeness to the man had blinded him to exactly how special and respected.

A high-standing member of the Council had stood up and spoke in a monotonous tone about Mr Lloyd's achievements and contributions. Hunter didn't hear a word of it. He stood there, hands shoved deep in his coat pockets, a sad smile as he remembered their own toasts to him.

Later, when every softly spoken conversation was exhausted, the heartfelt (and perfunctory) toasts made, Hunter and his friends escaped back to Astley Manor.

Hunter went and locked himself in his library. It seemed wrong that they still hadn't read through all of the papers Brian had left them, especially today. He was still sitting up in the early hours of the morning, matching information in Brian's work to his own collection.

"Shit." No, no, no. Hunter took a deep breath and rubbed his weary eyes, as though it could remove the revelation. Shit. Hunter jumped up, running through the sleeping house. "James!" He shouted, taking the stairs three at a time, "James!"

James came staggering out of his bedroom, just as Hunter reached the door, looking still asleep in his loose pyjamas. There was movement in the corridor as Sophie ran out, wrapping her dressing gown about her slim figure, a look of fear on her face.

Seeing her, Hunter suddenly remembered that the last time she was woken in the middle of the night had ended disastrously, and he felt a brief stab of guilt.

"Attack?" James asked, breathless.

Hunter shook his head. "Shadow." The single word managed to break out, and Hunter took a deep breath, "Brian's work, he was tracking the awakening of a Shadow."

"You're sure?" James asked, definitely awake now.

"Unfortunately, yes."

"Wait, what's a shadow?" Sophie interrupted, calmer now she knew there was no immediate danger.

"A Shadow Witch," Hunter began, fighting down his own fear. "The most powerful witch - in a class of their own. But they are rare, near unheard of, there's only been two in recorded history."

"But it's still a witch. The MMC can stop them?" Sophie asked, still not grasping the significance of the title.

Hunter shook his head. "This is magic without limits, the last Shadow Witch to gain a hold ended the Dark Ages and unleashed the chaos of the medieval witch-craze. Society crumbled through fear and witches gained positions of power, free to slaughter thousands. They turned their own hunted existence to their use, accusing and murdering innocent victims, all in the name of the good lord."

"So this is a big deal, then." Sophie replied flatly once Hunter had finished.

Hunter checked his watch, 3am. It was definitely important enough to wake everyone up, but he'd still be hated for it.

"James, get on the phone to the Council. Hopefully the foreign delegates haven't left yet. Offer Astley Manor as a meeting place. I'm going downstairs, to see what my collection has to help." No, there'd be no sleep tonight. "Ah, Sophie, you can go back to bed, if you want."

"No, I'm awake now, I'll help."

Nine

The Council had done a good job at dragging witch-hunters into a meeting at such short notice. By midday Astley Manor was a hub of noise as over fifty witch-hunters of various nationalities gathered. At 2pm they all piled into the long hall, where Hunter went over all the details under the sceptical gaze of his fellow witch-hunters.

Outside the closed door, two people were left out.

"This is ridiculous, we should be in there." Sophie spat, glaring at the door that separated them from the meeting.

James shrugged. "I'm a first gen too, we're not permitted to attend witch-hunter meetings, except for exceptional circumstances." Yeah, but it was still a bitch. "Besides, we know everything Hunter has to say, and he'll tell us everything they say."

"It's still not as good as hearing it for ourselves. And if this isn't an exceptional circumstance, what is?!"

They waited impatiently for a good couple of hours, hearing nothing except the odd, inarticulate shout.

"Hunter said there were two Shadow Witches." Sophie said suddenly, making James jump. "But this morning I could only find writings on one."

James grimaced. "Not many people know about the second, some don't even believe she even was a Shadow. She didn't last long and it was all hushed up. Back in the 40s. I only know 'cos Hunter-"

James broke off and eyed Sophie carefully. "Ah, I'm sure he won't mind me tellin' you. His grandfather, Old George V, brought her down. Just wish we knew how. The old man's long dead and never spoke of it to anyone."

Just then, finally, the doors opened and the witch-hunters poured out, followed in the end by Hunter. Just one look showed how disappointed he was. Several witch-hunters hung back to share a few words of encouragement, but eventually they were all gone.

"I need a drink," Hunter muttered and slunk off to the kitchen to retrieve the much needed bottle of whiskey, and quickly poured himself a healthy glass full.

James and Sophie waited impatiently.

"Well?" James finally asked with exasperation.

Hunter took his time replying. "They've decided to do nothing."

"What?!"

Again, a pause. "Oh, they believe there's a Shadow Witch at least. Took long enough to persuade them on that. But they have decided that there is nothing more they can do - they are just going to keep on witch hunting until the Shadow Witch makes a move."

"Well," Sophie said hesitantly. "That's not too bad."

"Hah." Hunter grimaced, "They wouldn't change anything: putting more witch-hunters and Council staff on the case to track the Shadow down; they could increase communication between foreign MMCs; they could plan to unite all witch-hunters or at least form a plan of action in the case of the Shadow rising up. But no, they didn't want to take priority away from normal business!"

Hunter's rant left James and Sophie silent.

"The MMC in general may not be willing, but you've got me, as much as I can do." Sophie said with calm confidence.

"And me." James added. "And Charlotte is gonna help too, of course."

*****

Sophie carefully carried the mugs of coffee as she descended the dimly lit stone stairs. She hissed when the hot drink spilled onto her hand and swore under her breath. For the past week, since the disappointing MMC meeting, Sophie felt like she'd done nothing but traipse up and down carrying drinks and sandwiches, or reading old manuscripts. On the whole it felt like she was achieving nothing.

Hunter and James had been researching too, but also had the more interesting duty of travelling to meet sources. They hadn't taken Sophie, citing her inexperience, and needing to spread their resources as less than satisfactory reasons.

But today they were all in the Manor. They had found nothing more promising than Old George had killed the last Shadow Witch. Hunter reasoned that his grandfather's belongings might hold some secret, protection or a weapon perhaps? No one had looked at the Astley Collection in detail for years now, so today they were attacking it with a vengeance. And Sophie was playing the little tea lady.

"Hey, coffee." Sophie announced as she entered the library. She glanced to Hunter who was absorbed in his work, and the last mug of coffee she'd brought him sitting untouched and stone cold at the side of the desk. She sighed. "You know, I won't bother if you're not going to drink it."

Hunter looked up guiltily and took the hot, fresh coffee from her, overly alert that their fingers brushed at the exchange. Sophie seemed to notice it too, a faint rise of colour in her cheeks, and she looked swiftly away.

"Did you find anything new?" She asked casually.

Hunter shook his head, "Old George didn't believe in organisation. If he had a filing system, it wasn't one known to man. I'm struggling to find anything in his notes either."

Hunter sighed and leant back. Actually, he was discovering that he and Old George were alike in these traits. The only difference was that Old didn't have James twittering and moaning in the background, but somehow making everything miraculously work smoothly.

Sophie put her hand on his shoulder and leant forward to view the erratic notes, the papers weighted down with random objects of random interest. Her silky, dark brown hair fell forward, with a rich scent that Hunter couldn't help noticing.

"Well, we'll just have to keep at it," Sophie replied, turning to face him as she spoke.

Close to, her hazel eyes had little flecks of gold. She was as harsh as ever, but that was something Hunter had come to accept. But he couldn't help but stop with the realisation that she was beautiful. It did tend to make work awkward.

"Thank you." Perhaps he shouldn't, but he couldn't break that gaze.

Sophie frowned. Her expressions were always so slight, but they were familiar now, the way her down-turned lips were set, the delicate crease of her brow.

"Look, Hunter…"

"HUNTER!"

They both jumped. There was the sound of trainers down the stone steps.

"Intercom, James." Hunter chided.

"Yeah." James answered offhandedly. "Anyway, I just got off the phone wi' bloody Americans. Good news, they're taking this seriously and want to act. Bad news, they want to run the show."

"Ugh, I can't be dealing with them." Hunter muttered. He couldn't deny that having them on board would be a huge help, but having them in charge - America's way of running things resembled a big, bolshy kid with all brawn no brain.

"More good news," James added, waving some paper in the air. "The Germans sent this through on the fax just now. I had some friends in their Council dig up anything from the 1940's that could relate to the previous Shadow Witch. They found some letters they thought might help."

"Good, good." Hunter replied, interested now. "If you'd do the honour, James."

James grinned then read out the short letter.

"'Bericht. Wir haben schließlich befindet sich die-'"

"Wait, what?" Sophie interrupted. "In English?"

James stared at her accusingly. "You don't speak German? Shame. Things tend to lose something in meaning in translation."

"James," Hunter said in a quiet, warning tone. He'd had to put up with James being unnecessarily nasty to Sophie ever since she turned him down. Hunter had had enough.

"Fine." James grunted, then translated as he read, speaking quickly in a dull voice. "'Report. We have, in the end the items. You may report with confidence that we are ready for the first attempt - everything is very promising. Herr Braun and Herr Hartmann have proved helpful in the deciphering of the information and breaking the protection around all the items. Herr Braun demands that more witches are brought in to help with the final incantation. I suggest that Hartmann lays immediately to go hunting more witches. We wait for your orders. Herr Richter.'"

"Richter? What do we know about him?" Hunter asked, the name completely unfamiliar to him.

James shrugged. "Not much, he was part of the group that researched occult powers for the Nazi party."

"And the others mentioned, Braun and Hartmann?"

"Braun was a witch - he got caught and killed after the war. Hartmann, well, from this it sounded like he was a witch-hunter."

Hunter frowned. "A witch-hunter working alongside a witch?"

"The Second World War was a pretty big deal, Hunter, I think the lines of what was right and wrong got skewed, especially working for the Nazi party," James responded succinctly. "But what do you think? All this magical activity and research shortly before the arrival of a Shadow Witch in Britain. Could they have found a way to raise a Shadow Witch?"

"It seems perfectly possible." Hunter took the copy of the letter and read it for himself. If the Germans found a way to raise a Shadow, the witch could have awoken anywhere in the world; in England, alone and unprepared, relatively easy prey for the local witch-hunters...

Hunter sighed, putting the letter on his cluttered desk, he didn't voice his thoughts.

Ten

"You really think she's up to it?" James asked.

Sophie gave an uncharacteristically inelegant snort of derision at his question.

The three of them were in the Land Rover, Hunter driving, James in the passenger seat, and lowly Sophie sitting in the back. Hunter's hands tightened on the wheel as he concentrated on the road rather than answering James' question.

"Hunter? You think she's ready?" James persisted. They were on their way to a raid, it would be Sophie's first time coming up against witches as a witch-hunter, and typically James wasn't happy about the idea.

Hunter shrugged, not the most positive gesture, he realised. "She's done her training well. Besides, would you rather she have her first time out at Hallowe'en? She needs to operate in the real world."

"Hallowe'en is nearly a month away, she has time for more preparation if you're not sure," James cautioned.

"She, she, she!" Sophie suddenly spat. "I'm sitting right here. Why don't you ask me if I think I'm ready?"

Hunter shot her a look in the rear-view mirror. "Because, my dear, we know exactly what you think. You've been champing on the bit these last few weeks, dropping increasingly obvious hints every time a job comes through from the MMC. If you had your way, this would be your fifth raid, not your first."

Sophie sat back, a rather superior smile on her lips. For once she didn't rise to the ribbing, she was getting what she wanted right now.

"This isn't my first time, anyway." Sophie suddenly said, breaking the silence. "Brian took me to a raid. Although I wasn't allowed to actually do anything, just watch him and the other witch-hunters outnumber and overpower a small coven."

"Yes, well, I'm sure Brian knew what he was doing." Hunter replied distractedly. "And I doubt you'll be doing anything this time, there are more than enough higher gen witch-hunters to deal with the threat. But you need to learn, so you are going to stand there and do exactly as instructed, even if that is to stand and watch; even if that is to return to the car and wait. Understood?"

When Sophie didn't respond, Hunter met her gaze in the rear-view mirror. "Understood?" he repeated, harder.

Sophie looked away. "Yes," She said quietly, gazing out the car window.

Hunter suddenly turned off the road onto a dirt track. The Land Rover lurched over the rubble and potholes for a few hundred metres until a big black Jeep and a blue Volvo came into view. Hunter pulled up next to the other parked cars, and as if on cue, every car door opened and seven people were clambering out.

"Hey, Hunter!"

Hunter squinted in the low afternoon sun. He smiled, matching the voice to the driver of the Volvo. "Toby! It's been a while. How's the wife?"

"Bloody chitchat. You're late, Astley." The driver of the black Jeep grumbled, interrupting the polite exchange.

Hunter grit his teeth against the insulting tone, his eyes suddenly cold. "I would say that we are right on time, Mr Halbrook. We were told to meet at 4 o'clock."

"Yeah, so good of you not to arrive a minute earlier than necessary, Mr Astley," he responded, deeply bitter.

Hunter sighed, it hadn't been his choice to have Gareth Halbrook on the team, but the MMC had assigned him, and there was no getting rid. Oh dear, best to just get the job over and done with quickly.

"Who have you brought?" Hunter asked, nodding casually to the two young men that had climbed out of the black Jeep.

"Matt and Dave Marshall, 3rd gens. I took over their training after their old da got killed a few months ago." Gareth responded unenthusiastically. "What about your guys?"

"James Bennett and Sophie Murphy, both first gens."

The Marshall brothers looked at them all silently, their faces betraying an unprofessional interest as they

94

glanced at Sophie. Sophie grimaced in disgust and shifted closer to James.

"Firsts? You brought a couple of firsts?" Gareth demanded, spitting slightly in his anger. "What the hell use is that?"

"They are fully-trained, Mr Halbrook. I don't have time to argue with you," Hunter said, fighting to keep his calm. "Can we please get on with the planning?"

Gareth folded his arms and glared at Hunter challengingly. "Whatever you say, sir."

Toby, the Volvo driver that had greeted Hunter, now stepped forward, shaking his head at the conflict. He laid a large sheet of paper on the bonnet of Hunter's Land Rover.

"The MMC have received reports of frequent gatherings of witches at a nearby wood. They meet and cast at sunset, I know, predictably dramatic. We estimate four to six witches, none showing extraordinary magic." Toby reeled off the information he had collected while at the MMC headquarters earlier that day. He leaned over Hunter's car, indicating the paper. "This is a map of the surrounding area. The clearing is here, about a mile into the wood. Unfortunately there's no natural barriers, so we'll just have to surround them and hope they don't break through."

Gareth leaned over the map. "We don't know which way they'll be arriving, so we should wait until they start casting before we move into position. It is more dangerous, I know, but it's our best chance of surrounding them. We could probably park up here to wait."

He jabbed at a spot on the map, then looked up, and shrugged. "But what do I know, I'm just a 4th gen with twenty years' experience, obviously not enough to be in charge. What do you think, Astley?"

Hunter frowned. He really didn't like the fact that his 7th gen status gave him superiority over more experienced witch-hunters. And he liked it even less when odious individuals like Gareth Halbrook held it over him.

Hunter gazed at the map, uncomfortably aware of the silence and the eyes all focussed on him. Damn Gareth. "No, I agree. Let's move out." He finally admitted through gritted teeth.

Gareth turned back to his jeep, a smug smile on his face, with the two Marshall brothers in tow.

"Want a lift, Toby?" Hunter offered. "I don't think your little car is up to a cross-country jaunt."

Toby folded the map and smiled. "Sure, why not. If it isn't the witches that kill me, it'll be your driving."

The four of them piled into the Land Rover, James now demoted to the back seat with Sophie.

"Behave yourselves back there, children," Hunter teased as he started the engine.

He smiled as Sophie swore under her breath, then put the car into gear and leapt across the field, following the tracks made by Gareth, racing after the black jeep towards the dark shadow on the horizon.

"Who the hell invited Gareth Halbrook?" James demanded, holding on tight against the bumping, speeding car. "Of all the witch-hunters they could've assigned, why that git?"

Toby smiled sadly. "It's Hunter's fault."

"What?" Hunter asked sharply.

Toby spared a quick glance around the other passengers and propped himself against the door, grimacing as the car lurched over uneven ground. "The buzz at the headquarters is that Hunter is too big for the Council."

"What's that supposed to mean?" Hunter asked, not liking the sound of it.

"Ah, you know the influence you have. Enlisting Sophie here, determining where she carries out her training. Your preferential treatment of James, that he gets to see more than some higher gens, that you refused to let the Council reassign him last year. The fact that you refuse to take on 1st gens for training, and your lack of attendance at the headquarters. Christ, even Charlotte was promoted quickly beyond her years on your advice."

"That isn't fair," Hunter said, when he'd heard enough. "My influence? I will act how I see fit, but I am loyal to the MMC and they will always have the final decision in everything. This 'influence' isn't of my making - it is the Council's way of treating me."

"I know Hunter," Toby said in a pacifying tone. "But you are the miraculous 7th gen, no one knows what you could be capable of. The Council wants to keep you sweet, but at the same time they doubt their ability to control you. Hence, Gareth Halbrook. They're giving you your birthright to lead, yet proving that they are in charge by making you work with that arse."

Hunter sat in silent thought, staring straight ahead to the looming woods where the black jeep had already pulled up.

"You'd think," Hunter said quietly. "That the Council would have more pressing issues to deal with than these ridiculous games."

Nobody replied, it was obvious where Hunter's thoughts lay - the MMC were spending time and energy worrying about non-existent problems, when there was one very real, glaring threat of the re-emergence of the Shadow Witch about which they did nothing.

The uncomfortable silence was ended by their arrival at the edge of the woods. Everyone clambered out again, the day still too hot to stay inside the stationary vehicle. There was nothing left to do but wait for the sun to set and the witches to make their move.

Sophie was sitting against the trunk of a shady oak, wondering how best to phrase her thoughts.

"So... what have these witches done? To upset the MMC?"

Hunter stopped his pacing and looked at her. "What do you mean?"

Sophie kicked the dirt in front of her. "I was just curious as to what their crime was. The usual murder and mayhem?"

"Their crime is that they're witches, love."

Sophie looked up at the sound of the rough voice; Dave, or Matt, she couldn't remember which, was looking back with a laughing sneer.

Hunter ignored the Marshall boy. "They've done nothing that we know of, yet. This is a pre-emptive strike."

"So... they're going to be punished, possibly killed, in case one day they are guilty." Sophie frowned, trying to get her head around the concept.

Her statement stunned everyone. One of the lads guffawed; and Gareth gave a sharp 'ha', throwing Hunter a dirty look. Even Toby and James looked mildly disgusted at the insinuation.

Poor Hunter felt a flush of embarrassment at his trainee's ignorance. "You're doing it again, Sophie, you're thinking they are like humans. They are witches, it is inevitable that they'll do evil - should we wait for innocent people to get hurt before we act? And we can't punish them for things they haven't done - we'll just bind them and process them, and set them free. I doubt it will be necessary to kill them."

"More's the pity," Gareth grumbled.

Hunter's head snapped round at this. He knew that some of his colleagues harboured this opinion privately, but no one ever voiced it. Apart from this bastard.

"Oh, I know you champion the non-violent outcomes, but be serious, binding witches wastes time and resources. Honestly, the only good witch is a dead witch, and if I had my way..."

"I know what would happen if you had your way," Hunter warned. Oh, he knew. He was very much aware of Halbrook's trigger-happy reputation. "But I'm in charge here and we're doing it my way."

"Sorry, sir," Gareth responded sarcastically. "Don't worry about me, I'll take care of myself. You just watch your witch-loving first."

Hunter took a stride towards him, not sure if he was going to shout, scream, plead or punch. Maybe all four. But he stopped in his tracks. There was a faint hum of a whisper in that part of his mind that was always alert and dominant.

"It's time," Hunter said, suddenly realizing the sun had dropped below the horizon.

Nearly a minute later, Toby, the Marshalls, and Gareth cocked their heads as though hearing something faint.

On a sudden impulse, they all rose, quickly inventoried their defences and weapons, then looked to Hunter.

"Let's go," he simply said, striding into the shadow of the trees.

Sophie and James came close behind, followed by Toby. Gareth and the Marshalls left a long, defiant gap, yet followed Hunter's lead.

Hunter walked into the deepening gloom of the evening woods, his senses sharpening with every step. He was aware of the six bodies behind him, their warmth, their separate breaths and footsteps. He was aware of the building throb of magic ahead of them, drawing closer he could sense the individual rhythm of the spells that bubbled up and called to him. He couldn't read any violence from it, and repeated this observation aloud for the others.

"There are four witches actively casting, but keep alert." Hunter added in a low voice, "This should be an easy one, so let's try to keep it civil."

This last part was directed obviously at Gareth, who pretended not to hear.

"Please don't say it'll be easy," James muttered, sharply knocking the nearest tree.

The others smiled nervously at his remark, then turned in the direction of the threat. Hunter signalled them to move into position, muttering last minute instructions and warnings, before allowing them to leave.

This was the part he hated most, he reflected as the other witch-hunters disappeared into the forest, he was personally brave and would risk his life as and when required. But to send others out to risk theirs always made him nervous, and yes, a little bit guilty.

But, as the boss of this operation, he could at least put the weakest in the safest place. New girl Sophie was behind the first line, Hunter voicing that they needed someone to stop the witches breaking through their circle. The excuse fooled no one, but Sophie, excited to be on her first real raid, didn't argue and docilely fell into place behind Toby and Matt Marshall.

In formation they moved forward on silent feet, led on by the promise of firelight ahead.

It was as Toby described, a clearing only 20 metres in diameter, a fire cracking, in its light four figures moved. Physically, the witches were unremarkable and unrecognisable as something other than human. But there was the aura of something more.

There were two female and two male witches, looking, in an ordinary light, as two couples having a bonfire night.

Hunter took a deep breath and stepped into the circle of light.

"I am Hunter Astley, by the Malleus Constitution you will surrender now to my authority to be bound and registered." He called out, confidently, "If you refuse to come quietly, we are empowered to take any means necessary."

Out of the shadows, the rest of the witch-hunters stepped forward, guns raised.

The witches, who had gazed at Hunter curiously as he approached, now reacted as they were surrounded. The men instinctively moved to protect their partners. Their breath quickened and anger and fear tainted their expressions.

"We have done nothing wrong," The nearest male witch spat.

"Nevertheless, by the Malleus Constitution, all magic must be bound," Hunter replied formally. His eyes flicked up to Gareth, who looked bored and impatient. "Please, you are outnumbered, just surrender."

The male witch exhaled, his shoulders dropping with resignation. "There are worse things than death." He muttered, then raised his hands. Everything went black.

In a blind panic, Dave Marshall fired his gun into the darkness. There was a scream as the bullet ripped through flesh and bone.

"Stop!" Hunter shouted, furious at the witch-hunter. His 7th gen eyes piercing through the magic, he could see the blurred shape of the male witch still in front of him. Hunter gritted his teeth and launched himself at the witch, moving with unnatural speed, he knocked aside the witch's sluggish reaction and dealt a blow of such strength the man fell to the floor.

Around him the darkness faltered and faded, the light of the fire and stars perceivable again. Hunter looked around quickly, the male witch lay incapacitated at his feet. Off to his right, there was the result of Dave Marshall's nerves - Toby lay on the floor, trying to stem the blood flow from his arm.

One of the female witches jumped at the opportunity and ran at this weak spot in their circle.

"Stop!" Matt Marshall stepped into her path, but a wave of magic sent him flying unceremoniously head over heels, hitting a tree with a sickening thud.

"No," gasped Hunter, as the witch faced the last witch-hunter blocking her escape.

Deadly pale, Sophie raised her gun and fired.

The female witch gave a strangled cry and stumbled, falling to the forest floor. Blood blossomed a startling red from her chest and she could be seen to be gasping erratically from pain and shock.

Hunter ignored the unconscious male witch at his feet, he ignored the two remaining witches that now surrendered to James and Dave Marshall; Hunter stepped past the bleeding female witch and straight up to Sophie.

"Are you ok? Did she hurt you?" he asked, his voice low and desperate. He quickly glanced over her, there

103

wasn't a mark on her, but Sophie was white and shivering. Hunter slowly moved closer, reaching out and gently prying the gun from her hand. "Sophie, it's ok, it's over. You did good."

Sophie's eyes snapped onto his, wide with panic and adrenaline. She was drowning in the shock of the moment and Hunter felt a sudden urge to reach out and save her, hold her close and protect her. An urge that he fought.

Hunter stepped away from Sophie, unsettled by this sudden intimacy. He forced himself to look around and assess the situation.

Toby was sitting on the mossy ground, staunching a wound in his arm. He looked bloody and pale, but otherwise ok, with Dave Marshall kneeling next to him, babbling out incoherent apologies and excuses.

The scene re-lit the anger Hunter felt towards that arse, Gareth Halbrook, who with his trigger-happy team had ruined a smooth operation. Hunter turned to look for the offending git and was surprised to see Gareth walking calmly in his direction.

Hunter opened his mouth to shout and course his anger, when Gareth raised his gun and shot a single round at the injured female witch at his feet.

Hunter felt a shock of fury as her heartbeat and irregular breathing left the web of sounds.

"You murderous bastard. What the hell did you do that for?" he shouted.

"Put her out of her misery" Halbrook replied roughly, staring challengingly at Hunter.

"She could have survived - there was no need."

"Survived for what? The taxpayers to pay for us to keep her. No thanks. As I said, the only good witch is a dead witch." Halbrook glanced over his shoulder at the living witches, obviously picturing the same fate for them.

Hunter shook with rage, completely unable to speak after such a statement. He felt a restraining hand on his arm and turned to face a pale and worried James.

But James was looking at Gareth Halbrook. "Mr Halbrook, take the prisoners to HQ."

Gareth frowned at James' assumed authority. Damned first gen, suddenly getting bossy, just because he was the famous Hunter Astley's friend. "Look 'ere-"

"No, you look," James interrupted. "You and your boys take care of the witches, 'cos I don't want t'leave Toby in your hands. And if you know what's good for you, those witches'll arrive at HQ without a single mark on them - got it?"

Gareth ground his teeth, obviously weighing up the cost of saying what was on his mind at this point. But in the end he grumbled something inaudible and stomped off, jerking his head at the Marshall brothers. The three trouble-makers left, herding the two witches before them, Halbrook picking up and carrying the still-unconscious male witch.

James finally looked to Hunter. "Come on, let's go. I'll help Toby, if you help Sophie."

Hunter nodded, and finally dragged his attention back to his other colleagues. He watched James help Toby to his feet and support him, they set off in the direction of the Land Rover at a slow, stumbling pace.

Hunter turned to Sophie, who looked still pale, but more composed now. "Can you walk?" He asked, uncertainly.

"I'm not an invalid," Sophie snapped in a reassuringly offended manner. Her cold, sharp self returning now the immediate shock was passing. "Don't treat me like a damsel in distress."

Hunter shrugged, his mind too full of other concerns to be too relieved that Sophie was okay. They walked together, slowly following James and Toby back to the car. The four travelled in near silence. When they got back to the Land Rover, they found Gareth's Jeep already gone. The four witch-hunters climbed back into Hunter's vehicle and made their way back to the road, slower this time, Hunter driving more carefully so as not to jostle Toby. Again there was silence.

They finally turned onto a dirt track and the headlights lit up Toby's blue Volvo. Hunter pulled up next to it. Again, James took charge.

"Right, I'll drive Toby up t'hospital, then I'll head to the MMC - it's late, but I want to follow up Halbrook. Go home Hunter." After helping Toby into the back seat of the Volvo, James spoke quietly to Hunter. "Just keep an eye on Sophie. I think she's hiding her shock."

Hunter nodded, clapping his friend on the back and climbing back into the driver's seat of his Land Rover.

James said something privately to Sophie, wearing a serious expression, then got into the Volvo.

"Are you sure you're ok?" Hunter asked again, as Sophie climbed into passenger's seat beside him.

"Yes," she replied exasperatedly. She then stared resolutely out the dark window.

106

Hunter nodded again. Good, silence, that was fine.

They were roaring down the motorways, Hunter showing a certain disregard for speed limits, when he decided to speak.

"What did James have to say?" He asked, his voice suddenly seeming loud after the silence.

Sophie finally looked at him, but only briefly. "Nothing," she muttered.

Hunter was unconvinced. He had an odd feeling that just as James had asked him to watch Sophie in case she went into shock, the annoying Yorkshireman had asked Sophie to keep an eye on Hunter's mood after the run-in with Halbrook.

They lapsed into silence again. Then Sophie shifted uncomfortably. "Does it get any easier?"

"What do you mean?"

"Killing witches, does it get easier with time?" she asked, turning to face him.

Her hazel eyes burnt with the pain of the question, she seemed shaken, yet strong. Again Hunter felt that dragging sensation that he should hold her, that he could keep her whole.

A horn blared as he nearly collided with another car. Hunter snapped his attention back to the road, his hands tightening on the wheel. He could feel the pressure of the seat belt against his shoulder, and was bizarrely glad for such a restraint.

"No, it doesn't get easier," he replied honestly, staring resolutely ahead. "And I don't want it to, I don't want to be like him, like Gareth."

No, Hunter couldn't imagine that killing witches would ever mean nothing to him, or worse, that he'd take some sick pleasure from it.

It seemed to take forever to get back to Astley Manor. It was midnight by the time they pulled up the gravely drive to the big old house. The lights were still on, the fires lit ready for their return, and they gladly went into the warmth.

"Are you sure you're ok?" Hunter asked again, as they stood together in the hallway.

Sophie gave him a withering look. "Goodnight, Hunter."

Hunter watched Sophie walk away from him and move up the main staircase, heading straight for her room. He didn't want her to be alone; he told himself that she shouldn't be alone after such a day. But a part of him knew better. Oh god, he was in trouble.

"Sophie…" He called out, then thought better of it as she paused on the stairs. "Sophie, tell James that I don't need babysitting."

Eleven

Hunter sat alone with Sophie in the library, books spread out down the long table. He was aware of the furtive looks she kept shooting him. Despite the dark matter of the books around him, and the oppressive environment since his discovery, Hunter found this amusing.

Out of the corner of his eye, he saw her look again. This time he smiled. "Is there something I can help you with, Sophie?"

A blush crept over her cheeks. "What's it like?" she blurted out.

"What is what like?" Hunter asked, smiling at the vague question.

Sophie closed the heavy volume in front of her, Hunter saw the faded title: 'Witches and their hunters of the Romanic region: 16th century study'. Hmm, poor girl, no wonder her mind was wandering.

"What's it like, being a further generation witch-hunter? Do you feel differently from other people?" Sophie asked, using more detail this time.

Hunter thought about this, not for the first time. "Honestly, I don't know, I've never been normal so how can I compare? Perhaps I should ask if you feel different from a 7th gen."

Hunter smiled teasingly, but closed his book, willing to be more serious. "Everything I do feels normal and natural, but sometimes I see other people's reactions when I move too quickly, or show too much strength and so on. So surely there's something abnormal enough to catch their attention. Does that answer your question well enough?"

Sophie said nothing for a minute or two, staring into space with her own thoughts. "And... what is it like when you perceive magic?"

Hunter looked at her with askance.

"What, I'm not allowed to be curious because I'll never experience it?" Sophie demanded.

"Fine," Hunter said, leaning back in his chair, his gaze fixed on his new charge. "It's... it's like a headache, or at least it used to be when I was younger. A niggling, burgeoning activity that can be mistaken for pain. But you can train yourself to concentrate on it, read it, taste it. Every strain of magic has a different taste, or rhythm. As soon as a witch casts, I can tell what the magic is for, even who cast it."

Hunter stopped, grimacing at his own description, as though he were a connoisseur of art or fine wine. Had he really gotten so expert in his dark career?

"And it improves with each generation?" Sophie encouraged. "What's the furthest you've perceived magic?"

Hunter nodded, oh yes, as the famous 7th gen he was born with unfair advantages against the witches.

"The furthest?"

Hunter broke off as James made his entrance kicking the old door open so he could carry in the coffee tray. "Couldn't find Charles, so made it meself. Hope you like strong coffee."

"James, what would you say is the furthest I've felt a casting?" Hunter asked mildly. "Ten miles?"

James slid the coffee tray onto the busy table. "Ten easy. Remember the one in Hereford last month, must've been fifteen."

Sophie just nodded, silently taking in the information.

"You know this is summat you'll never experience." James said, casually cruel. "Not jealous of our Hunter, are you?"

Sophie gave him a haughty stare in reply, flicking her brown hair back over her shoulder.

"I'm curious, surely that's allowed," she said coldly. "Besides, this all sounds a touch too close to magic."

The effect was instantaneous. James stopped laughing at her and Hunter's smile froze.

Sophie seemed to realize the severity of what she'd said, and started stuttering. "Look... it's not... I didn't mean-"

"Never say that." Hunter warned in a chilling tone, his eyes furious. "How dare you even make such a heinous association?"

Hunter stood up so quickly, Sophie flinched as though expecting him to hit her. But Hunter kept his fists by his side and turned towards the door, needing space.

"You don't seem to realize how offensive your ignorant comments are, Sophie. And showing me up in front of Gareth Halbrook and his cronies last week – no, I haven't forgotten that. I've been pretty damn lenient with your whole attitude, but one day you'll have to deal directly with the MMC, and they won't be as understanding." Hunter took a deep breath, the worst of his rant over, but his eyes still blazed. "You said you wanted to be a witch-hunter. Well, you've got to be in this a hundred percent, you've got to sort your attitude out and stop this... this sympathy for magic. Or you need to walk out that door right now."

Hunter motioned towards the open library door. The room was silent and motionless again.

Sophie was tense, her hazel eyes cast down. But the fact that she wasn't biting back showed that there was at least some truth in Hunter's outburst.

"I'm here. I'm in," she eventually muttered. She looked uncertain for a minute, then quietly turned back to her book.

Hunter felt no joy in setting Sophie straight, he felt strangely empty after letting loose, and now stood by his chair, not sure what to do.

James on the other hand felt perfectly comfortable in giving Sophie a disgusted look before turning to Hunter. "You know, this coffee isn't working. How 'bout we knock off and head down t'local instead?"

Hunter looked at his watch and sighed. "Yeah, sure. I've time for a drink before I take Rachel to dinner."

The two boys promptly left the library to get their coats, and Sophie (who was unsure whether or not the invitation extended to her) sat alone, quietly reading the dusty volume before her.

Twelve

There's something about Hallowe'en that seemed to excite the witchkind. Perhaps it was to do with the pagan fire ritual of Samhain, their magic amped up by something earthly. Or maybe it was just the thrill of moving openly, while a world of naïve victims actually celebrated their existence.

If it was anything like last year, it would be uncontrolled chaos. Even the newspapers and the general ignorant public had suspected something after the wave of identical murders that the MMC hadn't been able to completely cover up.

So all the witch-hunters were on high alert. Even if they looked foolish…

It was early evening, but it was already dark outside. Hunter stood close to the warm fireplace, the old house did get cold once autumn came round, and Charles worked overtime keeping it pleasant for the Astley family and their guests.

Making the effort for Hallowe'en without sacrificing style, Hunter was wearing a tasteful black suit with a long black cloak and a white mask covering half his face.

"Let me guess, 'Phantom of the Opera' meets Armani?"

Sophie stood in the doorway, looking so fantastic that Hunter was left momentarily speechless. She smiled in her own grimacing way and turned so that he could see her outfit, sultry dark red tones on black, close fitting to her slim curves, the long skirt slit to the thigh. She'd done something clever with her make-up to make her face pale, but still stunning. Oh yes, and rubber fangs sticking out over her lower lip.

"Sexy vampire?" Hunter asked needlessly.

"Well, I was going to be a witch, but I thought that would be too ironic," Sophie replied, lisping slightly over the false teeth. She shook her head and pulled them out, "Hm, I don't think I'll be wearing these all night though. I don't see why the MMC want us to dress up and go out like a group of normals, when there's going to be so much activity."

"Ah well," How embarrassing. Hunter had previously told Sophie what she needed to hear. "We have no intel on what will happen where, so the MMC likes its witch-hunters to be on the move, in the thick of it, so they can act immediately." This was repeating his earlier statement. The next bit she may not like. "But the dressing up like a prat is my idea. You know, to fit in. Come on, we've got to pick James up. Are you kitted up?"

Sophie's frown deepened, but she nodded. Hunter had provided her with a personal handgun and small dagger - where she'd managed to hide them in that figure-hugging ensemble though... Hunter snapped back to attention.

"Yes, James, let's go."

They took the Land Rover, the 4x4 equipped with protective charms and the boot stocked with the tools of their trade. Sophie jumped into the passenger seat, and they drove in familiar silence to James' modest house.

And out came a pirate. And hadn't he put the effort in: hat; dreadlocked wig; bandanna; skull shirt with homemade tearing; long shorts (again with the tears); and lord knows where he got the long boots, probably the same place he got the courage to wear them.

"Nice outfit," Sophie said carefully as James clambered into the back seat.

"Thanks," James replied, shooting a victorious look at Hunter.

Friend or not, what an idiot. "James has worn the same outfit for the past three years. He got a bit of a Johnny Depp fixation when we were at university." Hunter told Sophie, with a commendably deadpan expression.

"Hey," James shouted from the back. "I didn't have a 'fixation'. I just really enjoyed Pirates of the Caribbean, and I dare you to say Captain Jack wasn't cool."

"I agree," Hunter conceded. "He was cool. Five years ago. Now it's only obsessives with no personal, original imagination of their own-"

And Sophie sat quietly, staring out the car window at the moonlit fields and cottages. Over the past couple of months she'd gotten used to the two boys bickering like an old married couple.

Soon, the view out her window was the stream of slow-moving cars and the bright lights of bars. The sound of music and the laughter of the revellers hit the car. Hunter parked up and they all got out and made their way into the nearest bar.

"I know the MMC like us to be out and ready for action, but this?" Sophie asked, looking around with distaste.

"Look, most activity isn't until midnight. Sure, most witch-hunters will be sitting in their cars, drinking coffee and trawling the streets. But the MMC doesn't care if we have one last party before getting on the job, as long as we stick to soft drinks," Hunter replied seriously, after just handing out the first round of beer and wine. "You never know when it's your last call. Besides, look around, we're surrounded by victims. So relax, enjoy yourself for once."

Hmm, although she didn't go wild, Sophie gave in to the party spirit and, after another glass of wine, she even deigned to smile every now and then.

James, with the odd confidence bestowed by wearing a pirate costume was enjoying the dancefloor a bit too much for his sober state. Hunter had the fun of watching his friend make an arse of himself - he'd remind James of these embarrassing intervals at later times.

Every now and then, bonny girls walked over to try and get Hunter to join in the dancing, but he declined and the girls were often chased away by a cold glare by Sophie.

"Not getting jealous, are you?" Hunter laughed, leaning in towards her. "And I thought you didn't like me!"

Sophie, stiff and frozen as ever, turned away from him. "I just don't think it is right. We're working."

Hunter smiled, she didn't change. He reached out and placed his hand on her lower back, he felt a thrill when she didn't pull away. He got the sudden image of trying to gentle a wild horse that could turn and kick you in the head at any moment.

"Come on, it's twenty to twelve. Let's get the dancing pirate and go." Hunter said to her quietly.

The trio emerged from the warm pub into the brittle, clear night. The first stop was the car, where they threw in their extraneous costume and pulled out a kit bag each. Then they meandered without any particular aim to the edge of the night scene. It was here, where drunken revellers stumbled away from their pubs and clubs, making their way home, it was here the witches were likely to hunt their prey.

All they could do was wander the streets, waiting for something to prick Hunter's senses. Hunter glanced at his watch, nearly midnight. A sigh escaped him, this time last year he was being torn apart by all the magic being used. He was pretty confident that he could sense magic within a fifteen mile radius. But still nothing. What the hell was going on?

"Hunter."

118

Thirteen

"Hunter?"

Sophie's voice came so quiet and she sounded so scared, Hunter felt fear grip his heart as he turned. Sophie stood there, looking strangely stiff.

"Sophie, you alright?" James asked, looking at her carefully.

Sophie didn't reply. Her eyes closed and slowly a smile creased her red lips. There was a bristling of energy about her.

"Oh shit." Hunter grabbed James and pulled him back from her, expecting an outburst.

But nothing flamboyant happened, yet. The energy of magic was so high that Hunter felt deafened by it.

Sophie opened her eyes, unseeingly. By the lamplight her hazel eyes were clouded over with what looked like thick white cataracts.

"Sophie, what are you doing? Can you hear me?" Hunter said loudly.

Sophie tilted her head slightly and looked at Hunter with an expression of curiosity. "Sophie can hear you.

119

But unfortunately can't answer, you see she has given control of this vessel to me tonight." The voice was Sophie's with something of a deeper tone, throbbing with power.

"You're a witch. She wouldn't - Sophie would not help a witch." James almost shouted back.

Sophie turned slowly to look directly at James with those clouded eyes. "Simple boy, I don't need a willing soul, she still fights my presence - quite annoying, very stubborn. But I am stronger. Shall I prove it?"

Her hand threw up and James gasped, dropping to his knees and clawing at his constricted chest, unable to breath, his heart struggling to beat.

"Stop!" Hunter screamed. "By the Malleus Maleficarum I command you to stop."

"For now." The voice replied, dropping Sophie's hand. Immediately James began to gulp down a lungful of air, his face red. "If he speaks again, he dies."

"What do you want?" Hunter asked, forcing himself to remain calm. What else could he do, a witch was attacking his two friends.

"I want to see you, you who discovered my return; you Astley, whose family seems tied to my fate."

"Shadow... The Shadow Witch." The words whispered from his lips in disbelief. Hunter had a right to be scared. "Then here I am, leave my friends out of it."

Sophie smiled. "I have not come to kill you, not tonight. But now I see your weakness, I see how close you are to these insignificant mortals. I see into this

120

girl's thoughts and I see what pain I could inflict by killing them instead."

"No, you can't. I won't let you."

"Ah, now we come to it, Astley." The Shadow Witch spat his name out with such hatred, as though they had cursed his existence in their heart every day. "Can you stop me? You are a remarkable young man, I am sure. But now, I stand before you as vulnerable as you will ever find me. I am so strongly within this girl for this brief time - shoot her, kill us both."

Hunter raised his gun, pointing the barrel level at Sophie's chest. Yes, Sophie was just one person, with her death she could spare hundreds, possibly thousands of lives. His hand was steady, which was a miracle in itself.

No, he was not a murderer, not for the greater good. And he couldn't sacrifice Sophie, of all people. He slowly lowered the gun.

Sophie smiled, clouded eyes still fixed on Hunter. "I will make you regret your weakness, Astley. She will die."

"Don't you dare hurt Sophie, or I'll make it your regret. Now relinquish this girl." Hunter said fiercely.

There was one last ghost of a smile on Sophie's lips and then she crumpled. Hunter grabbed her, barely slowing her fall as Sophie hit the pavement. James, who had been hovering uselessly, now dashed to her side.

"She's still alive," James said, having checked her pulse and breathing. He glanced up at Hunter. "What on earth was that about?"

Hunter was equally confused. If that had been the Shadow Witch, what had been the point of contacting Hunter? No information given on either side, no deaths despite the threats. Surely they hadn't wished to just turn up and gloat in a big bad clichéd way.

"I don't know." Hunter responded. "But let's get Sophie back to the car."

James picked up the three heavy kit bags, and Hunter gently lifted Sophie's unconscious form. Although his senses were on high alert, Hunter felt no trace of magic remaining in the girl.

Back at the car the two men struggled to get Sophie onto the back seat.

"Shit!" Hunter jumped and swore as his mobile rang suddenly. He muttered at his own nerves and answered it sharply. It took a moment to understand the fast, panicked voice on the other end.

"Hey, slow down. Now what's happened?" Hunter asked, still not sure who he was talking to.

"They took her, the witches took her, I thought this place was protected, Hunter. But the shadows grew and wrapped around her and then Charlotte was gone."

Charlotte. Oh no. No, no, no. When the Shadow Witch had said 'she' would die, they had meant someone more important to Hunter than even Sophie.

"Look, Steve, we'll get her back, I promise you."

"If anything happens, I'll hold you responsible."

The line went dead. Hunter sat in a state of shock.

"Hunter," James' voice broke through the haze.

"Get on the phone, alert all the witch-hunters, the MMC, everyone. We need to find where she's been taken." Hunter said, suddenly spurred into action.

"Hunter." James repeated calmly. "Sophie's awake."

They both twisted in their seats to face Sophie, who was sitting straight and strong again. Looking into her eyes, although filled with panic, they were back to their cold hazel depths.

"The witch, I didn't let her, I tried to stop her but she was so strong." She looked down at her hands, flexing them, as though confirming her own control over her body again. "James, I-I'm sorry. And Hunter, it's all my fault. I could feel her, she sifted through my thoughts and memories and I was powerless to stop her. I showed her Charlotte."

"We don't blame you," Hunter said quickly, not sure if it was true. "We need to get moving, to find her before..."

His voice trailed off, so he started the engine.

"We don't even know where to start." James reasoned.

"Actually." Sophie said quietly, surprising the guys with a brief smile of pride. "The Shadow Witch was so preoccupied, she didn't notice that I could get into her thoughts. I saw a village church, it was a St Peters. It's not much to go on, but if all witch-hunters head to the nearest one, we've got more of a chance."

James was already on the phone, repeating Sophie's words to the Council. Hunter slammed the car into gear and sped off, ignoring every traffic rule. James kept his mobile glued to his ear and spewed out directions to Hunter to their nearest St Peters. But soon

123

it was unnecessary, as the miles flew by and they drew closer, Hunter could feel the pull of magic, telling them that this was the place.

They had all fallen silent by the time they had pulled up outside the church. It was a small, stone-built with old leaded windows. It was a lonely little building in a forgotten village.

The two men got out of the car and Sophie made to follow them.

"On no, you don't, you're staying in the car." Hunter said, blocking her way.

"Hunter, I'm a witch-hunter, I'm coming." Sophie responded, trying to push the car door out of his grip.

"No. The Shadow Witch has gone after you once already - stay in the car where you're protected."

Reluctantly, Sophie agreed. James pulled the kit bags out the boot. Hunter grabbed his stab jacket, pulling it on over his shirt. He took a deep breath, well, this was it.

"Hunter." Sophie grabbed his sleeve as he moved to leave, then pulled him close, pressing her soft lips against his, the scent of her skin and perfume. She released him slowly, reluctantly. "Come back alive."

Hunter staggered back and followed a silent James up to the church door. He glanced back once, unable to see Sophie's face clearly in the dark car.

At the church door, James turned to him. "Now what?"

Oh hell. They had never faced anything this big, for someone they cared so strongly for. Was this what it felt like, to know death waited impatiently for you?

124

"We go in," Hunter replied, meeting James' knowing gaze. "It's been fun."

They might die here tonight, but they both knew that they would never turn back. Hunter went first, pushing his weight against the thick wooden door. Inside the church was dimly lit by candles along the aisle and eaves. It was quiet, filled with shadows, empty of life. Hunter stepped cautiously up the centre aisle; there was something at the altar.

She lay as though asleep, her beautiful face serene, her arms by her side.

"Charlotte," Hunter whispered as he forgot all his caution and rushed up to her, desperate for her to respond. He reached out, now scared to touch her, her cheek felt warm against his hand. "Charlotte."

His hand traced her chest for any heartbeat, but stopped as he felt the soaked material of her black jumper. Blood stained his fingers. "No," he growled, anger and sorrow firing up within him like never before.

"Hunter," James hissed.

Hunter turned and immediately saw what had gained James' attention. Out of the shadows, black-clad figures stepped into the candlelight until a dozen witches faced them.

Hunter welcomed them. A raw fury filled Hunter's heart and soul. He would die and be with Charlotte again, but he would take as many of these bastards with him as possible.

"Come on then!" He screamed, raised his gun and fired. There was a rumble and a crack and the world seemed to be torn apart. The twelve witches were

125

thrown off their feet and back with a force against the stone walls and pillars. A fierce tempest whipped through the church, shaking it to its foundations. Masonry dust shook from the walls and rafters and suddenly great chunks of torn wood and stone were falling all about them.

*****

James opened his eyes, the world had not ended and he was somehow still alive. Ugh, bloody battered, but alive. The old church was nothing but rubble. He got slowly to his feet and looked around. The witches were barely visible beneath the stone, immobile limbs sticking up in awkward places.

Half fearful, James turned back to face where Hunter had been standing. The altar was still there, with Charlotte laid out serenely, Hunter standing over her. They were miraculously untouched, with only the faint layer of dust to show that they had been part of the scene. How the hell?

*****

"We need to talk about what happened," James said seriously. They were perched on the church wall and the first people from the MMC were just arriving.

Hunter remained silent, staring into the dark countryside.

"Hunter, I think the MMC will notice the church, they can count too - two of us against twelve witches that appeared out of nowhere. You're gonna have to talk to them. But first, we need to work out what happened." James paused for breath. He'd been expecting to die tonight - he should have died tonight. "That much power, it had to be the Shadow Witch, but

126

does that mean she's playing with us, or she wants you alive for some scary reason. Did you feel her presence, her magic?"

Hunter shook his head, no he hadn't felt anything, nothing except his own anger. And now he felt dead inside. "Let's go home," he muttered.

"We've got to stay, to help the Council. We've still got work to do."

"I don't bloody care!" Hunter shouted, getting fired up again, "The Council can go f-"

He jumped down from the wall and marched off. James had to rush to catch him.

"Ok mate, we'll deal with them later. But I'll drive."

Fourteen

It was dawn by the time they got back to Astley Manor. The trio shivered against the cold of the morning as they staggered into the entrance hall. There they stood, all unsure of what to do, how to act next.

James was the first to speak, his voice shaking with his own sorrow. "Hunter... do you want to, er, talk?"

"Will talking bring Charlotte back?" Hunter asked in a dead voice. His tired eyes looked up at James. "No, I didn't think so. I don't want to talk."

Hunter sighed and pushed past the others, disappearing into the recesses of the mansion.

Sophie went to follow him, but hesitated, every part of her uncertain. "Should I... is there anything I could do?"

"No," James snapped, then shrugged. "Sorry. But I think we should leave him for a while."

They stood in the hall for several long, silent minutes before James broke the silence again. "Perhaps you should just go to bed, you've had one hell of a night," he suggested, moving off up the staircase himself. One hell of a night for all of them. Christ.

Hunter had wandered into the sitting room, where a fire crackled in the grate. He'd been standing here only twelve hours ago, yet so much had happened.

"Oh, so you all decided to come back then?" A familiarly sharp voice came from the doorway, "I swear you use Hallowe'en as an excuse for all night frivolities, as Young did."

"Not now, mother." Hunter said through gritted teeth as he turned to face the bitter little woman.

"Oh dear, what happened?" Mrs Astley asked, somehow managing to make a possibly caring question sound harsh and spiteful.

"Charlotte. They killed Charlotte." Hunter turned away as his eyes filled with tears. Oh God, why her? He felt as though he'd lost a reason to live. The Shadow Witch was right about him, he was weak because he cared.

Mrs Astley sat down and looked at her son carefully. "Charlotte? That black girl you were infatuated with at university? Well there's no point blaming yourself, everyone dies and you know that."

"I do blame myself, it's my fault, mother. All because I loved her." Hunter felt a pang of regret, he'd never openly told Charlotte he loved her. He had stood back and watched her marry someone else and never said a thing. There was no point lying about it anymore.

"Don't start fretting over it, George. Anyway, she would never have been a suitable wife. Good heavens, could you imagine a coloured mistress of Astley Manor?"

Normally Hunter would ignore any and all comments from his ignorantly racist mother, no matter how foul, but anger still throbbed in his veins.

"Shut UP, you miserable old bag. Charlotte deserves respect, and as master of this house I will throw you out if you do not hold your tongue!"

Mrs Astley looked affronted, unused to her son being so reactive. She stood up suddenly. "I will not be spoken to in such a manner. Have Charles send tea up to my rooms. And we shall speak when you have calmed down and remembered your manners."

Hunter watched his mother leave the room. She was an irritating, narrow-minded...

He took a deep breath, his mother had never liked Charlotte, so her reaction hadn't surprised him. What was surprising was the raw energy of anger that refused to leave his otherwise numb body. Even though he'd not slept that night, he did not feel tired. He wanted to run, to fight, to do something other than give in to grief - and this anger whispered to him that he could. Yet his legs seemed not to respond.

He didn't know how long he stood there alone, leaning against the fireplace, his knuckles turned white in their fierce grip of the mantelpiece. But he couldn't feel it. He could not feel the heat from the fire burning his legs. It seemed that nothing now registered beyond the forlorn pounding of bitterness and repetitive thoughts that filled his mind.

"Hunter?" Sophie's voice broke through as she hovered by the door. But the figure by the fire made no comment, nor even recognised her presence. "George, please."

Sophie moved quietly towards him.

"She's dead," Hunter said in a harsh burst, finally turning to face Sophie. "Charlotte's dead. I couldn't save her. Never, never has my job - if I can't protect those I love… And I'm up against a Shadow."

"You should have killed her when she was in me. You could have ended it right there."

When Hunter looked at her he was surprised to see guilt and sadness in that normally cold face and icy hazel eyes. "I could never have killed you, though."

He stepped forward and took her in his arms, his lips pressing against hers, driven not by lust but utter despair.

Sophie pushed him away immediately, and when she spoke there was a warning plea in her voice. "Hunter, don't."

Hunter paused, his thoughts catching up with his actions. But his heart was beating and his breath coursed his lungs. This he could feel. He stepped towards her again.

"Then tell me you don't want me." He said softly, wrapping his arms about her elegant frame. His lips found hers again, and this time he felt Sophie yield to his embrace.

*****

It was the morning after the night before. That's how they described it, wasn't it? That period of time when rash, passionate actions were shown by the harsh light of day, provoking regret, guilt, and possibly embarrassment.

131

Hunter awoke early to a still-darkened room. He felt oddly calm, as though the stress, grief and rage of the last two days had, if not dulled, been pushed back to a more manageable perspective.

Hunter shifted his body slowly to sit up. In bed next to him Sophie was still sleeping soundly. He watched her for several long minutes, even in the half-light before dawn she was beautiful, and there was something softer, more serene about her face while she slept. He supposed it had to do with her chill and sharp intellect being reserved for dreams and out of his reach.

He moved slowly so as not to wake her, slipping out of bed and pulling on any old clothes before going downstairs. The rest of the house was still sleeping and as Charles hadn't lit the morning fires yet, the Manor was cold.

Hunter made his way to the kitchen for his first cup of coffee. He sat at the counter, nursing the steaming mug. He waited for the regret to kick in. In general Hunter enjoyed women and never worried about hurt feelings, he never hung around long enough. But Sophie was, well, a friend - and in a moment when he'd been mad with loss he had used her.

Although ashamed about the circumstances, he didn't regret it, nor did he want to scarper. He hated to admit it, but everyone had been right: he wanted her, cold, unyielding, frustrating Sophie.

Strangely he did feel guilt. That after professing to love Charlotte for so long, he suddenly dared to have a new focus in his life when he should be concerned with mourning.

It was over an hour later when Hunter gained company. Sophie hovered in the doorway.

"Morning," she said quietly, for once looking completely uncertain.

"Morning." Hunter echoed.

Sophie made herself a drink then sat opposite Hunter, her gaze averted. They sat in an increasingly uncomfortable silence.

"Look," Hunter finally started. "I wanted to apologise. My behaviour yesterday was unforgivable; I should never have taken advantage of you like that. I'm sorry."

"Oh." The single sound was the only reply Sophie could muster. She stared down at her hands, frowning as per usual.

'Oh'? Hunter was used to much wittier and informative responses from Sophie. He didn't like not knowing where he stood with her, he'd rather face her anger than try to be sufficed with a little 'Oh'.

The silence grew and Sophie offered nothing more, her face dark with her private thoughts. Oh dear, this was uncomfortable, bordering on embarrassing. Hunter didn't deal with that sort of thing, especially when work was likely to be involved. If Sophie didn't want him, Hunter would have to rethink this living and working arrangement.

Sophie stared into her steaming coffee, her fingers gripping the mug so tightly that they were turning white.

"That's fine. I understand that you just needed a distraction. So glad to prove useful," she finally answered bitterly, her eyes snapped up to him, cold and furious.

Hunter was a little shocked by her response and sat quietly, his early morning brain trying to catch up. And poor Sophie took his silence as agreement. She sighed, muttering something beneath her breath and sliding off the stool, only thinking of taking her coffee to the privacy of her own room.

"Is that really what you think?" Hunter asked, standing up to block her way out of the kitchen. "That you were just convenient and distracting?"

Sophie reluctantly met his gaze, her anger fading and replaced by what had caused it - fear of the unknown.

Hunter reached out, gently catching her by the arm to stop her from bolting. "I'd never dare think so low of you, Sophie. In fact, the truth is that I think about you more than I should, and I am only sorry that it took the shock of hallowe'en to make me act."

Sophie just continued to stare up at him, her breath increasing in rate, as her eyes dilated as her agitation grew. Obviously Hunter's new answer was no more welcome than his previous one. But then it was suddenly as if she made a decision, to take the risk and the consequences. Sophie leant in closer towards Hunter and kissed him hesitantly.

Sensing that she was no longer about to hit him or storm out, Hunter kissed her back, pulling her in til he could feel the warmth of her body and -

And then he pulled back sharply, swearing and shaking his hand where he'd spilt the hot coffee she'd been nursing so protectively. Hunter shook his head at

134

how smoothly that had gone, then chuckled at an afterthought.

"James is not going to like this," he said guiltily, not wanting to think how uncomfortable his best friend would be feeling. Hunter smiled at Sophie, taking her hot drink from her and setting it firmly on the side before trying that kiss again.

Fifteen

The next few days were a blur. There were the inevitable visits by the MMC. They questioned Hunter and James over and over about Hallowe'en. Poor Sophie had been grilled by several 'experts', trying to understand the Shadow Witch; whether Sophie was in danger; even whether Sophie was dangerous.

The Council had finally been scared into action, pulling people off mundane tasks and setting them to research and defence. When they came to Astley Manor with a long list of work for the resident witch-hunters, Hunter set his mother on them; they got the hint and didn't come back.

Hunter wasn't ready to face the world and didn't have the energy to survive it. He would happily have disappeared into nothingness. Only his new closeness to Sophie made him want to live.

Then one morning Hunter, Sophie and James finally left the Manor, all three dressed in black. It was a cold November day, with the first proper frosts of the year. Hunter felt Sophie shiver and he held her closer as they all stood in the graveyard, a silent crowd gathered, their breath fogging over the prayers.

It wasn't that long ago that they'd all been standing over another funeral, when Brian's death had seemed the worst thing to ever happen.

The crowd slowly departed, people stopping to say their own goodbyes, and to console the inconsolable widower. Hunter looked up. Steve stood by the graveside, his tall, thin figure swamped by the heavy black coat, his eyes so red from crying.

"Steve, I'm so sorry." Hunter said, finding himself walking up to Charlotte's husband.

Whack! Hunter recoiled in shock as timid Steve punched him squarely in the face. Through watering eyes, Hunter saw Steve rub his sore knuckles.

"You have no right to be here Hunter!" Steve shouted, ignorant of the other mourners that turned and stared. "It's all your fault - you got her into witch-hunting, you were supposed to protect her. Leave. If I ever see you again, I swear I'll kill you."

Hunter was dragged away by both Sophie and James. He shouldn't have expected anything else from Steve. But now that Charlotte was laid to rest, Hunter was ready to get back in the action. Everything would work out, it had to, especially when he had James and Sophie still with him.

*****

That night, Hunter found the concept of sleep impossible, even with the comforting warmth of Sophie beside him. He watched her sleep with a quiet fascination. She seemed so peaceful, until the early hours of the morning, when the rhythm of sleep became

137

disturbed. A pained expression crumpled her face and she struggled against the bedclothes.

Suddenly, Sophie jolted awake with a strangled cry, sitting up in bed now, her body tense and trembling.

"Sophie, Sophie, it's alright." Hunter murmured gently to her, his hand placed against her flushed cheek. "Did you have a nightmare?"

Sophie, eyes wide with panic, her gaze roving over him in slow understanding as she tried to shake off the images. "Just a dream," she muttered, forcing herself to be calm. "Just a dream."

"Do you want to talk about it?" Hunter asked.

"No," Sophie replied shortly, lying back down.

Hunter sighed. "It might help," he insisted. Yes, it might help him pass the hours until dawn, when he no longer had to pretend to need rest and bed.

Sophie looked at him in assessment. "It was nothing, it…" She broke off, unable to shake the possessing dream. "Fine, the truth. We were at the graveyard, like today, and the Shadow Witch was waiting at the gate. She was wearing Death's garb and called to you. I begged you not to go, but you walked through the gate with your head high and your stupid pride. Then, knowing that you were dead, and I alive - in the dream I was distraught, I… I…"

Sophie stopped, struggling to find words to express her feelings. "It was a physical, inescapable pain. And I hated you for making me grieve your death."

Hunter remained quiet for a while, taking in this open answer. "It was just a dream. Probably set off by the funeral today."

138

Sophie frowned, forever fighting with herself, and building up the courage to say what was on her mind. "I don't want you to fight the Shadow Witch."

"What?" Hunter laughed, surprised by this sudden, ludicrous request.

"You don't have to go up against her. There are a hundred other witch-hunters that can face her," Sophie argued, in a quiet voice that was already defeated.

"Sophie, don't be ridiculous. How can I turn my back on the biggest threat of our time? I'm one of the best witch-hunters out there, if I don't stop her, who will?" Hunter argued back, logically.

"But if you face her you will be killed."

Hunter hesitated in his response, feeling a faint wave of foreboding. He shrugged it off. "That was nothing but your dream, Sophie. I may actually survive this thing, trust me."

Sophie propped herself up on her elbow in a sharp movement, her whole body emanating anger. "No, it's not just my dream, Hunter. Why don't you listen to me? I've seen inside the mind of the Shadow Witch, I've seen how she wants your death above all others, how she's imagined it a hundred different ways. She is your Death and you march proudly and stubbornly towards it."

Hunter was temporarily silenced by this revelation. "You never said -"

"It never seemed important." Sophie bit back. "But does it make you reconsider?"

"No," Hunter replied quickly.

Sophie hissed in disgust and rolled away from him. She lay still for so long that Hunter began to think that she'd fallen back to sleep.

"You awake, Sophie?" He eventually whispered.

"Yes," she snapped, remaining stubbornly turned away from him.

"Sophie, this is who I am. I cannot turn away from this fight, it's against my nature," Hunter said seriously. He reached out and stroked her back gently, frowning as she flinched away from him. "You wouldn't love me if I were any different."

The scene seemed to freeze. Neither of them had mentioned the 'L' word, nor even allowed themselves to think it in their most private thoughts.

"You're right," Sophie replied, finally turning to face him. "How I wish you were any other man right now, one not cursed by the Shadow Witch. If you should die, it would cut me down also."

Sophie reached out, her hand tracing his face, committing his features to memory. "Promise me you won't die."

Hunter smiled, then pulled her close to him, lips brushing her hair. "How I wish I could promise that."

Held close in Hunter's arms, Sophie slowly fell back to sleep, gentle and dreamless. Hunter sighed, the same foreboding reawakening in him, that all this was a temporary happiness.

"I am afeard. Being in night, all this is but a dream, too flattering-sweet to be substantial." He muttered to himself, unable to smile at the fitting words. Ah, was all this a premonition of the end, rushing up to greet them.

*****

Sophie dragged her bag down the wide main staircase, she hated getting Charles to carry her stuff when she could do it herself.

Hunter glanced out the window, checking for her taxi. "You're sure about this? The MMC can send someone."

Sophie dropped her bag by the front door. They'd already been over this. "I know, but I need to do this. If the Shadow Witch goes after our families, I want to be the one to protect my mum."

They had no idea where the witches would hit next, and it was logical that anyone connected to Hunter and Sophie were in danger and should be protected.

"I could come up with you." Hunter said, pulling her close.

"You have enough to do here." Sophie argued, pushing him away.

Hunter turned to pick up a small wooden case, about the size of a shoebox. He pressed it into Sophie's hands. "Now, the protective amulets will work best in the furthest four-"

"Corners of the house, and as many doorways and windows as they'll cover," Sophie finished impatiently, taking the heavy box. "James has already drilled me on this."

"I know, I'm sorry," Hunter apologised. Suddenly interrupted by the sharp blast of a car horn outside. Well, here as her taxi, come to take her to the station. "I'll miss you," he said seriously.

"Good," Sophie replied, finally deigning to smile and kiss him lightly before lugging her stuff to the waiting car. She opened the door then stopped, turning to look at Hunter with those fierce eyes. She hesitated, as though she wanted to say something, but in the end just frowned and got into the car.

Hunter watched as the taxi pulled away down the gravelled courtyard and then off down the long drive. Sophie was right, there was work to do, and she had been trained well over the past six months, she'd be ok.

James was waiting in the library, and it was easy to see he was annoyed. Hunter couldn't blame him, it must have been awkward working around Hunter and Sophie lately.

"She gone?" James asked gruffly.

"Yes. Anything to report?"

"Nothing new." James sighed, "All authoritative figures in Britain are under MMC security, America and Europe are following suit. Russia's still not on board."

James handed Hunter some papers. "As for our own work, a name popped up. Sara Murray, she was the 1940s Shadow Witch. Born 1916 in North England, died 1945. No known descendants. Sorry it's nothing useful."

Hunter flicked through the papers, taking in only a few words. What was the point? So far, being better informed had not helped them against the witches. What was the Shadow Witch waiting for?

"Never mind," Hunter muttered. "When are we next on duty?"

"Thursday. We're on rota along with John Ward for seven days on Downing Street," James replied.

"Right." That was better, being out there, even if they weren't prepared. "But, James, this time no swearing at every politician you meet."

Sixteen

It was nine o'clock in the evening, outside it was dark and miserable. Inside the building, the empty corridors were dimly lit by the glowing exit signs. The Council staff that were on night-shift were tucked away in little rooms, with no idea anything out of the ordinary would occur.

The light flickered and the shadows began to move, sliding across the plastic floors and twisting up into a physical being. The female figure was dressed entirely in black, a heavy hood pulled up, completely shadowing the face from view. The witch walked through every defence and protection as though they did not exist, and the guards were not alerted to her presence. She let herself into an empty office with a gloved hand. On the glass door, bold letters spelt out 'Bound Witch Office'. The witch swept past the empty desks to a door at the back of the room. It was locked, but the witch had taken the pains of procuring the key, there was a faint click as it unlocked.

Beyond the doorway, a short series of steps led to the floor of a long dark room, with the faint gleam of metal shelves that stretched into the darkness. The witch knelt down and pressed her hand to the concrete floor, a crack of pale light appeared, then ran the distance of the room, criss-crossing and lighting the bottom rows of a hundred shelves.

Everywhere there were amulets and stones, each containing the essence of power from every bound witch of the past 150 years. All irretrievable, irreversible - unless you had the key.

The witch-hunters had been greedy and naïve in keeping these amulets - did they think they could use the stolen magic of witches somehow? Or had they never found a way to truly destroy them? It didn't matter either way.

The witch took out a bronze dagger. The security of this place was pathetic. The MMC had thought themselves safe, they had thought themselves very clever indeed. There was only one key in the world and they'd given its secret location to one trusted member of the Council.

Did they really think this was protection enough against the Shadow Witch and her followers? It had taken a while to track down, but the key, the bronze dagger, was hers.

The witch knelt down again and drove the dagger on the throbbing light of the crack with all her strength. For a moment nothing happened, then the light flashed red and flared up from the floor, sparking and spitting. The light touched one amulet, then another, they all cracked with a piercing scream until the room vibrated with the sound of a thousand broken vessels.

Beneath the shadow of her hood, the witch smiled. All of her bound kin were free - let's see how the MMC would handle the mass uprising of all the quiet little witches locked up together in prisons in their hundreds.

The witch retrieved the dagger, her trophy, and turned to leave, her job was done. The only thing left was to leave her signature.

The Shadow Witch held her arms out, and felt a familiar rumble as her magic built up. With an almighty blast it was released, throwing aside concrete, brick and metal. The entire wing of the building was rubble, and the Shadow Witch was nowhere to be found.

Seventeen

The world was turned upside down. There were worldwide reports of mass breakouts from high security prisons. There were attacks on MMC headquarters and strongholds. The general public were driven into fear at the orchestrated and sudden violence, they struggled to explain it, grasping wildly at terrorism, or even more wildly, witchcraft as inexplicable occurrences happened in every town and city in the British Isles.

Hunter and James were dragged from sleep by an emergency phone call. The witch-hunter on the other end could hardly remain calm enough to pass on the message - the impossible had happened, a witch had managed to get into and destroy the MMC headquarters and now all bound witches in the UK were re-empowered. They acted in an organised manner, which meant they must have been planning this for a while.

Hunter and James raced to reinforce the nearest prison for witchkind. James drove, as Hunter's senses

147

violently sparked with the strength of magic that almost deafened him. Both were nervously aware of the enormity of what lay ahead.

The big grey compound was alight with fires and the glow of spells and illusions. The injured witch-hunters were being pulled back to relative safety, while the survivors fought desperately to keep the witches contained.

Hunter and James ran into the fray without a second thought. All about them, witch-hunters were firing into a half-illusion crowd of witches. Magic was flying erratically in every direction, spells to distract, spells to burn, spells to kill.

A burning block of stone suddenly flew into a dense area of witch-hunters, and there was screaming mixed with the thunder of collision. Hunter pulled James out of the way of flying debris.

"Get the injured to safety," Hunter shouted over the noise.

James nodded and headed into the bloody and broken mess. He wasn't a coward, but all 1st gens had their uses away from the actual battle.

Hunter turned back to the front. A black shadow was rippling and spreading over the ground towards them with an incredible speed. Hunter's sharp eyes broke through the haze to see hundreds of oversized spiders scuttling towards them.

"Spiders. Knives." Hunter shouted down the line.

The other witch-hunters didn't hesitate but pulled out long knives (and one or two swords). The wave of arachnids hit. Hunter slashed through the first wave with quick and deadly accuracy, no time to feel fear of the dog-sized spiders.

To his right he could see a witch-hunter fall to the powerful venom, and the spiders broke through to the second line. But he didn't have time to think about it, as more and more of the creatures scuttled on and Hunter fought to keep cutting them down.

More gun-shots rang out from the far wing of the witch-hunters, and the plague of spiders began to abate as their creators were killed. They had a brief chance to catch their breath, but Hunter noticed the thinning of the witch-hunter lines as casualties were pulled back.

They needed a miracle.

Everything got quieter, stifled and slowed. The world got darker, a darkness that even Hunter's eyes couldn't pierce. Hunter's heart pounded with fear as he felt a familiar rhythm to the blanket of magic. The Shadow Witch, it had to be.

There was a voice, muffled and just beyond hearing. Then everything switched back to normal.

The noise and the cold returned. Hunter looked about, trying to find an answer for what just happened, but the other witch-hunters appeared not to have noticed, or even been affected by the odd period.

A drop of cold water hit Hunter's face and he looked up. The previously clear night sky now rolled with thick, ominous clouds, tinged with colour. A storm was coming unnaturally fast.

Shouts rose up from the witch-hunters, bringing Hunter's attention back to the fight. Like an organised force, the witches threw out a thousand vicious illusions that swooped towards the witch-hunters.

There was a crack of thunder across the sky just as the wave of illusions hit. The line of tired witch-hunters wavered, and lesser gens attempted to fight the incorporeal monsters. With his highly trained senses, Hunter saw through the mass of illusion and saw the witches run away into a growing black shadow. His heart pounded again as they just vanished. That was impossible, witches couldn't physically disappear or transport themselves. The Shadow Witch. It was the only explanation.

Hunter snapped to as screams and shouts rose again from the ranks. He went to move but suddenly felt a stinging pain across his shoulder. He saw blood start to trickle from a shallow cut. Hunter looked up briefly. The storm clouds seethed and boiled and suddenly thousands of shards of ice were pelting down into the witch-hunters, cutting, slicing, blinding. The wind picked up, driving the sharp pieces harder against them as they started to run in every direction, slipping on the ground as it turned white beneath their feet, chased by the ice.

Eighteen

It was a sad dawn. Half of the witch-hunters had been killed, the rest were sporting various degrees of injury. No one had escaped unscathed. Word filtered through of similar results across the country. The MMC was in tatters.

Astley Manor had been converted into a makeshift headquarters for the MMC. After all, it was famous for housing and protecting seven generations of witch-hunters. No one wanted to face the fact that no protection had yet stopped the Shadow Witch.

Hunter limped through the busy rooms, noting that everyone was bruised, and sporting cuts and bloody bandages. But they were alive. That's what counted. They'd given some of the rooms over to casualties and the doctors and nurses they'd dragged in. Others had been designated as control and communication for the remaining rabble of MMC staff and witch-hunters.

Hunter was looking for someone in particular. James had come into his own over the past few hours, fielding calls, making arrangements for medical care, and keeping track of everyone.

Hunter found him as soon as he got chance to. "James, I still haven't been able to get in touch with Sophie."

It was true, since returning to Astley Manor that morning they had been trying to locate every witch-hunter - even 1st gens. Hunter had been trying Sophie's mobile and her mum's number all morning, both without success. In the present climate, and with Sophie's recent run-in with the Shadow Witch, this was very worrying.

James checked his watch. "You're right, there should've been contact by now. I'll have a couple o' witch-hunters up there swing by her mum's, check it out."

A witch-hunter came up, interrupting them. "Mr Astley, we've managed to track the Shadow Witch's movements."

Oh yes, even when James was the most competent person in the room, because it was his house and he was famously a 7th gen, everyone turned to Hunter as their general in this time of war.

"Go on then, give us the summary."

The witch-hunter shuffled his papers nervously, obviously too dependent on coffee. "The Shadow Witch struck us, er, the UK headquarters first. Then every European and the two African divisions within the next three hours. They report similar outbreaks.

"Then when night hit America, the Shadow Witch attacked their MMC, then Canada, Mexico, each South American division.

152

"We've warned the eastern MMCs, and Australia. But what they'll be able to do..." The witch-hunter finished, then stood there somewhat awkwardly.

"It seems impossible - one witch hitting every country in the world in 24 hours, and still being able to attack us back at the prison." James muttered. "How though?"

"Did you never wonder how Father Christmas did it?" Hunter asked bitterly, taking out his frustration on those around him. "It's a Shadow Witch, remember, magic without limits. I think she is very much capable of disappearing from one place and reappearing in another. And I think she can move others too - back at the prison I saw the witches retreating into a shadow and vanishing. And remember what Steve said - that the shadows grew and wrapped around when they took..." Hunter broke off, but after a deep breath continued. "That's how she was able to get into Steve's house, the MMC, how she took over Sophie - all those amulets, wards, protections are nothing to her. Because she can become nothing."

When Hunter finished, his pulse raced with the excitement of the revelation. Wait, excitement, shouldn't it be fear? But, whatever, he knew he was right, he had to be.

"But, if nowt can stop her, she could attack here." James voiced, trying to sound calm.

"No, I don't think so." Hunter replied, then hesitated, glancing at the witch-hunter that still hovered with them. "At any rate, they'll have to find us first. Can you check on the PM and royal family?"

The witch-hunter jumped with caffeine-heightened nerves. "We managed to relocate them before the witches hit London."

Hunter frowned, the man really didn't get the hint. "Then go help organising our forces."

They watched the man slink off. "Well?" James asked quietly.

Hunter led off to a rare quiet spot in the house, James fell into step beside him.

"I think Astley Manor is safe." Hunter confided in a quiet voice. "After all, Old George was linked with the last Shadow, and the Manor was never attacked, even after he eliminated her. I think the house has had more protections built in than anywhere else - the stones for instance. The fact that no witch has ever attacked the Manor."

"And you couldn't say this in front of t'other bloke?" James asked, completely unsure of why his friend was being so secretive.

Hunter shrugged. "There's something going on around us that I don't understand, and I have a feeling it's something that's no good. Something the MMC won't like, even if it aids us." Hunter shook his head, he didn't know how to describe it. "Besides, I don't want to raise false hope, I don't want the witch-hunters thinking they are safe, now that they are here."

*****

The next few hours passed in a haze of activity and breaking news - none of it good. Australia fell, despite the positioning of a small army at their MMC headquarters. Japan fell; China; Russia; India - with the witch-hunters nearly completely destroyed.

Reports came in from the battles that were still going on, with varying degrees of failure. But one thing was becoming clear, for some unknown reason, even when the witches were winning against the witch-hunters, they all pulled back like obedient troops and disappeared.

Which meant that this was only a brief calm and something worse was in store.

*****

"Astley!" A 5th gen witch-hunter called out. Hunter struggled to remember the man's name as he walked over.

Short bloke, looked about fifty, had the same stubborn air about him as old Brian had. Anthony Marks, that was it.

"I've just had the Americans on the phone. They're blaming us for the worldwide uprising of bound witches."

"What?"

Marks grimaced. "They claim that we failed in our duty to protect the Key."

"That's ridiculous." Hunter replied, angry now at their American cousins. "The key could have been anywhere in the world, in the deepest jungle, or buried in Antarctica for all we know. How can they blame us?"

"Because somehow their Council knew where it was. It was placed under heavy protection with an English member of the MMC - Mrs Charlotte King."

"What?" Hunter's voice came out louder than he'd meant, several people looked up at the shout. But Charlotte, his Charlotte? He couldn't believe that she

155

had never told him. But then, if she'd confided in him, Hunter would never have allowed her to take on the role of Key Keeper, it would make her a target for every witch - it had made her a target. The Shadow Witch, had she known and planned all this.

"Hunter."

Hunter looked up at the witch-hunter, but it wasn't he that had spoken. James came up behind him.

"Hunter, Sophie's missing. I've just had a call from a couple of our guys. They went to her mum's house in the Lake District, neither Sophie or Bev were there. They said there was no sign of a struggle or foul play."

Hunter had feared that this would happen, he'd been expecting it, he realised. He was tied to the Shadow Witch, and on top of all the violence and chaos, she was systematically attacking him where it hurt most.

"Where are you going?" James demanded as Hunter marched off.

"Where do you think? I'm going up there," Hunter replied, pulling on a coat and checking for car keys.

"Hunter, you can't. They might be waiting for you," James reasoned, then stopped, realising that particular argument wouldn't stop him. "Let some other witch-hunters go up and trace them."

Hunter looked at James ruefully. "I'm not sending anyone anywhere that I wouldn't go first. Besides, no one can feel the traces of magic better than me."

James grabbed his arm to stop him leaving, Hunter tried to shrug him off and got the surprise of mild James throwing him with some force back down the hall.

"Look, I know you're a bloody hero, we all do," James said angrily. "But it's tough shit, because right now you're the only man that can lead us. Sending people into difficult situations and trusting them is part of leadership. Get used to it."

The two best friends stood facing one another in silence.

"Don't try to compare this James," Hunter eventually spoke. "Because I'm not going to let the Shadow take Sophie, and I'm the only one that can bring her back."

As he said it Hunter knew that it was the truth, it wasn't just his ego, he actually believed that he could bring her back alive.

"Nothing you can do or say will stop me, James. I'm going, and I'd prefer not to have to break your nose to get there."

At first it seemed as though James wasn't going to move, but then he stepped aside, grabbing his own coat.

"No, you're not coming. It's too dangerous, and I need someone in charge of this place," Hunter argued immediately.

"Shut up, or we will fight. Someone's gotta keep you out of trouble. Besides, next to the rest of the witch-hunters here, I'm a useless 1st gen. Let's go."

Nineteen

It took them less than ten minutes to hand over control to the trustworthy 5th gen Marks; and to be in the Land Rover for a long drive north.

The roads were almost empty. The world had been shook by fear, a state of emergency had been announced and everyone stayed at home while official-types tried to recreate normality.

The two men drove non-stop to the Lake District in silence. Once or twice James attempted to engage Hunter in conversation, having the opinion that Hunter knew more than he'd let on. But Hunter remained in stony silence, paying full attention to the roads as they hurtled down them.

It was an early winter's evening and they were driving in near darkness now, the headlights cutting through the black countryside. Eventually they were driving down the familiar winding roads that led to the edge of Keswick. They were almost holding their breath as they turned the final bend to look on Bev Murphy's cottage.

Everything looked quiet and untouched. They kitted up and made their way down the path to the front door. It was unlocked, and when Hunter opened it, inside it was dark and silent. Hunter paused, but he couldn't feel any magic in the area.

He clicked the hall light on and the two men went into the familiar, modern interior of Bev's cottage. They did a quick sweep of the rooms. They were all empty, with no indication of where Mrs Murphy and her daughter were. The last witch-hunters to stop by had been right, there was no sign of anything happening.

Perhaps, perhaps Sophie and her mum had been out, and had either been taken or caught up in the fights. But Hunter fought back the fear of these mental images, he needed to stay focussed.

James was on the house phone to Astley Manor, clocking in and picking up any new reports. Hunter busied himself by going over the house again. By the front and back door he saw the amulets that he had given Sophie only a few days ago.

Hunter hesitated. Something pricked his senses. It was so faint that he could hardly feel it. He turned on the spot, then began to move slowly in different directions, even pressing up against the walls to try and find the source of the magic. But wherever he went, the magic got neither stronger nor weaker.

"James," Hunter called out uncertainly.

Suddenly he staggered, unbalanced, and the lights flickered and then snapped off.

Hunter waited, but couldn't sense anything else. He stumbled about the hallway, trying to find the light switch. Finally he felt it, he flicked the switch several times, but nothing happened.

"Hunter!" There was a crash and some strong swearing from James as he tripped over lord knows what in the dark. "Hunter, the phone's dead."

Hunter frowned, felt in his pocket for his mobile and pulled it out. The screen still glowed, but there was no signal.

By this time James had pulled out his torch and made his way to Hunter. "What do you think it is? Ambush? I knew we were walking into a trap."

"Shut up a minute," Hunter replied. In the silence, nothing disturbed his senses. "I can't sense anything."

"You mean there's no witches in waiting?" Asked James hopefully.

"No, I mean I can't sense anything. At all. There's no trace or residue. That wasn't magic." Hunter replied, knowing it sounded ridiculous. He didn't know how to explain it. He somehow knew that the earlier hint of magic was responsible, but the spell hadn't been performed here.

"The street lights are out." James mentioned, looking out the window onto an unlit world. "Why would witches knock out the power grid for the Lake District?"

"My honest opinion?" Hunter asked as James turned back to him. "I think it is part of something bigger. We need to get back to the Manor." He paused, pulling out his own torch, adding a little more light to the dark house. "Sweep the house for any clues Sophie might have left, then we go."

They kept together this time, twin beams of light flickering over every surface in a quick assessment of the cottage. It helped fight the fear of the incomprehensible happenings, to think, to move, to concentrate.

They'd just come out of Sophie's room after a thorough search, but finding nothing. Hunter stopped in the hall, he thought he heard, or sensed, a third person breathing. It was such a small sound, only half-heard that he wondered if it were his desperate imagination.

He flashed his torch down the corridor, but it was empty. About to confirm it as a trick of his nerves, Hunter felt his heart contract as the torchlight that touched the walls dimmed and became indistinct. It was as though a black fog was inside the house. As though the shadows were growing.

"James." His voice was strangled.

"What is it?" James asked in a returning whisper, coming back to him. But stared at the darkness with a sudden understanding.

"This is Hunter Astley of the Malleus Maleficarum Council," Hunter called out steadily. "We are here to demand the safe return of Sophie and Beverley Murphy."

Hunter drew his gun, holding it low. James kept close behind and silently followed suit.

There was an echo of humourless laughter within the confines of his own mind. Hunter frowned, not overly disconcerted, witches seemed to enjoy whispering directly into the mind as a means of terrorising victims and witch-hunters alike.

"You have no authority over me, Astley." The words cut into his mind, eerily with the effect of his own voice. "But I am glad to have found a way to gain your undivided attention."

Hunter glanced over to James, wondering if he too heard voices. But it was impossible to read his expression in the dimmed torchlight.

"If you want to see them again, come."

Hunter wondered at the command. He stared into the shadows that suddenly expanded, then stopped just in front of them. It was so persuasively solid, that Hunter had to stop himself from reaching out to touch the darkness.

"The Shadow Witch wants me," he said simply to James, and stepped.

If he'd been asked how he knew what to do, he couldn't have answered, in fact, the little voice of sense in Hunter's head was screaming at him as he stepped into the all-consuming darkness. It was warmer than he'd expected, and the shadows clamped onto him with a certain softness, muffling sound and blocking light, with all the effect of being wrapped in a huge black duvet.

The darkness faded to grey, and Hunter felt solid ground beneath his feet and cold air in his lungs again. He looked about, he quickly figured he was in an empty room. There was a dark window, a wooden door and a bare wooden floor, all lit by a single yellow bulb.

"Well, that was an experience."

Hunter span round, in utter shock to find James standing behind him. "No James, you shouldn't be here. Go back now."

"I go where you go, remember." James answered with a sorry shake of his head. "Besides, I think it was a one-way trip."

Hunter paused, suddenly paying more attention to their predicament. Hunter no longer had his torch in his hand - wait, hell, he no longer had his gun, knives, kit bag. His hands patted down his body, feeling the unnatural absence of weapons. Then his hand flew to his throat. Yes, there was still the metal chain and the old dog tags. Not that that was much comfort at the moment.

Another look around the bare room and Hunter noticed the lack of shadows. Whatever path had been opened was now well and truly closed.

James seemed oddly calm, accepting whatever nightmare he'd entered with courage. "Well, we've confirmed that the Shadow Witch can transport herself and others. Although I think I managed to gatecrash this one."

"Yeah, well, let's hope it's to our advantage," Hunter replied, pacing the room. He walked up to the window, it was large enough to admit a person if they could just open it. He pressed his hand against the cold pane - he could feel the rhythm of magic expertly woven over the glass and its frame. Even if they could break through the spell and smash the window, several iron bars prevented escape.

Not out the window then.

Hunter went to the door. Here there were no spells to keep them in, instead there was a heavy oak door with lock, and probably bolted from the other side.

"We stuck here?" James asked mildly.

"Looks like," Hunter replied, equally calmed by the knowledge that they couldn't actively do anything.

"Jolly good. How long do you think it'll be before-"

James broke off as there was the sound of a key in the lock. "Ah, perfect timing," he grumbled.

The thick wooden door opened and a woman stepped in. She took one (rather shocked) look at James and went out again, the door locked behind her.

"Short but sweet. Do you think they'll send us home now?" joked James.

They didn't have long to wait before she returned, this time with company. Half a dozen male and female witches came into the room. They took their cue from the original woman and surrounded the two witch-hunters.

"Which of you is George Astley VII?" The woman asked.

"I am." James piped up before Hunter had a chance to speak.

"Shut up with your Spartacus routine. I am George Astley, and I shall prove it if you doubt me," Hunter responded, defiance in his voice and steel in his gaze. "I want to see Sophie Murphy. Now."

The woman-witch smiled, almost bristling with the joy of having power over these defenceless witch-hunters. "You are in no position to be making demands, Astley. You will do precisely what the

Shadow Witch commands, and see only those she allows."

The witch nodded to her companions who stepped forward and roughly seized the men's arms, yanking them back. Hunter felt the sold touch of metal against his skin and the soft click as his wrists were handcuffed behind his back. He forced himself not to struggle or fight back, as much as his nerves screamed for action.

"Are the cuffs really necessary?" he asked, for the sake of asking.

"Let's just say we can't take too many precautions, where you are concerned," the witch replied curtly, then turned to lead the way out of the door.

Hunter and James were pushed into step, the witches always holding them, surrounding them.

"Hmm, I remember the last time I wore handcuffs - you remember Dervla?" James started prattling.

"James, I don't think this is the time for that particular story."

Twenty

They walked silently along a well-lit corridor. With the thick carpet beneath their feet and passing expensive cabinets and paintings it looked like they'd been brought to a very posh house, maybe even a manor. Hunter didn't know what to make of it, but he could hardly blame the Shadow Witch for wanting a luxurious set-up.

The lead witch opened a set of double doors, looking back at the prisoners with a poisonous smile.

They were taken into a large room. Black curtains were pulled across the large windows, the room lit with an ostentatious chandelier. There were long tables arranged in a horseshoe. Sitting around the table were at least twenty witches, looking very much like a civilised council - which was probably down to the suits that the majority were wearing, although the burn marks were not common in most boardrooms. All heads turned at the entrance of the witch-hunters.

Hunter could almost see the magical aura that bristled threateningly, at the same time he read the victorious feeling in their shining faces and quickened breath.

"Ladies and gentlemen. George Astley VII, as promised." A quiet female voice spoke, barely above a whisper.

Hunter looked at the speaker, sitting in a position of authority at the top table. She was the only one to wear a cloak, the dark material oddly mobile about her tall figure, the heavy hood filled with impenetrable shadow. Finally they were face to face with the infamous Shadow Witch.

Hunter gritted his teeth against the whole irritating stereotype of the situation.

"But you are not supposed to be here." The Shadow Witch said softly, raising a pale hand to indicate James.

"Yeah, sorry 'bout that," replied James daringly.

The whole room scowled at him, but let him be. They waited to follow the lead of the Shadow Witch.

"You wanted me, you got me," Hunter spoke up, "Now, I will only ask once. Give Sophie back to me."

The Shadow Witch stood up suddenly, and every eye was on her. "She is already here."

The Shadow reached up, and slowly slid the hood back, the dark shadow thinning to reveal the haughty beauty of Sophie Murphy.

Hunter felt a physical blow at this revelation and he heard James gasp behind him.

"Release her," Hunter breathed, his voice barely audible.

The Shadow Witch gently shook her head, "Not this time, Astley."

Hunter dared to look her directly in the eye. Her eyes... they were not clouded like the last time, instead they shone with familiar gold-flecked hazel depths.

The Shadow Witch smiled. "It's all over. The witchkind have won, the hunters are destroyed. There is no longer a need for disguise. So look, Astley, on the face that brought your downfall and curse your every mistake."

"No, you're lying." Hunter stood, heart pounding. It was all a trick, the Shadow Witch must have something yet to gain by possessing Sophie again.

There was a titter of laughter and scornful muttering broke out amongst the present witches. They were silenced with a single motion from the Shadow Witch.

"Why do I need to lie, Astley?" she asked innocently, "I have achieved my every desire. I have returned my fellow witches to their former glory. In fact, you join us on the night of our greatest achievement yet, perhaps you noticed a little power loss."

Neither witch-hunter responded, but the Shadow Witch didn't seem to expect an answer and continued.

"Yes, you can thank the Americans. Their MMC has been experimenting - unwisely, I might add - with magic stolen from witches. They managed to create a weapon that we would never have dreamt of. Used in a specific way, it could be directed to permanently disrupt every piece of technology, and with a little magical aid from me, it worked on a global scale."

Hunter thought back to the blackout, how he'd perceived something magical, yet distant and untouchable.

"Er, you expect us to believe that? 'Cos unless I'm mistaken this place is blazing with electric lights." James said suddenly, looking up at the gaudy chandelier.

The surrounding witches bristled at this, but the Shadow Witch just looked at him curiously.

A wave of power swept the room, blasting James off his feet and dashing him against the wall. He hit it with a sickening thud and slid to the floor. Hunter went to move, but strong hands held him in place.

"He doesn't learn, does he?" The Shadow Witch said coldly. "Tell him when he regains consciousness that there are more than enough witches here to light a few bulbs."

"Why - why destroy technology?" Hunter asked, struggling not to react.

"Because the Witches Council wished it so." The Shadow Witch replied willingly, looking at the faces of her associates. "The witches of today possess as much magic as they ever did. So why do we no longer inspire fear and worship, why are we ridiculed and cast aside as myth and fantasy? Because of the 'general ignorant public' as you so perfectly put it once. They are all so clever, so all-knowing, swallowing every story the MMC gives them.

"We have tried for generations to gain power politically, by mortal means. Yet witch-hunters persecuted all witchkind. So our new aim was to take the world all in one go.

"Imagine the fear and chaos when suddenly the world was plunged into darkness. There was no communication, suddenly no answers. It is in this chasm of disorder that those blessed with magic can step into their rightful roles above the ignorant and powerless masses."

There was a general cheer and a spatter of applause as the Shadow Witch finished speaking, the group of witches high on their recent victory.

"You're mad," Hunter muttered.

The Shadow Witch looked at him with an achingly familiar coldness. "Mad or not, we have won Astley."

"So what, you brought me here to do the clichéd gloat before killing me? Or do I get the option of watching you destroy everything first."

"I destroy only to create the world how it was meant to be. God Himself would do the same, if he existed." The Shadow Witch replied with cool logic, then half-smiled. "You have no idea how good it is to say all this openly after months of pretence and hiding around you."

She broke off, suddenly seeming to notice the rest of the room, hanging on her every word. "Take them away, I shall see them tomorrow."

She sat down and the two witch-hunters' audience was over. Hunter was shoved out of the room, while the unconscious James was carried by two male witches.

And it was back to the dull, empty room.

Hunter had been pacing the room for a while, when James finally groaned and opened his eyes.

"Wha' 'appened?" he asked groggily.

"The Shadow Witch threw you against a wall. How many fingers do you see?" Hunter peered at him carefully.

"Three."

"Close enough." Hunter helped him sit up, he back against the wall.

"Next time, remind me to stay quiet around her," James said, gingerly rubbing the back of his head. "Oh, they took off the handcuffs, that's nice."

Hunter sighed and sat down next to him.

"How bad is it?" James asked.

"Bad," Hunter admitted, thinking it an understatement.

"What are the witches planning to do?"

"Take over the world."

"Oh, that is bad. Did the Shadow Witch give a bad guy speech?"

"Oh yes, very impressive and clichéd - shame you missed it."

The two friends fell silent. It was James that spoke first, and this time he was much more serious.

"What about Sophie? You don't really think that she is the Shadow Witch - surely she's just possessing her again."

Hunter sat, looking quietly into space. The Shadow Witch was an evil entity. He wanted so much to believe that she was tricking them, that perhaps she needed to possess someone as the only way of taking physical form. That would mean that Sophie, his Sophie, was innocent and had loved him.

But there had been something about the witch, the clarity of her eyes and something else that made cold dread stab deep into his soul.

"I don't know, I honestly don't know," Hunter finally replied.

Twenty-one

The black window lightened to the cold grey of predawn. Hunter shifted, feeling stiff from his uncomfortable sitting position on the wooden floor. His eyes were gritty and he was tired - he and James had taken turns to keep watch while the other slept.

Hunter got up with a groan and looked out the window. It was still too dark to see anything. He traced the window again, reading the magic - it had a skill and a sense of logic that he'd not seen before. He knew that it was the Shadow Witch's handiwork. And that only she could break it.

"Is it tomorrow?" James asked with a yawn.

"I guess so," Hunter replied, looking at his watch out of habit. He frowned, the bloody expensive thing had stopped. It was stuck on a minute after 8pm.

They heard the bolt being drawn on the door and James jumped to his feet. The door opened and the same witch from last night came in with two male witches, standing with her like a pair of heavies.

"The Shadow Witch wants to see you," she said.

They both stepped forward, sharing the opinion that they might as well get it over with.

"No. Just you," she said, pointing at Hunter.

Her companions walked up to Hunter and, in a repeat of last night, he was abruptly handcuffed behind his back.

"Handcuffs again? You never told me Sophie was the kinky sort."

"James, I've already told you, not now," Hunter said, before being roughly pushed out of the room.

As the door was closed and locked behind him, he heard James call out, "What, no brekkie?"

As inappropriate as the situation was, Hunter couldn't help but smile. He'd never appreciated more, James' determination to have one last joke before death claimed them. He shouldn't be here, Hunter shouldn't have let him, he should have stayed in the relative safety of Astley Manor.

But Hunter never did have any control over James. It was maddening, how Hunter could walk into a room of the best witch-hunters and wave his 7th gen status, and they would usually respect, follow, obey etc.

But James? From the day he'd met him, James seemed to purposefully ignore and wind Hunter up, yet he always did the right thing.

Down the fancy corridor again, he was taken further this time. The lead witch finally stopped and knocked on a door.

A few moments passed, and then the door was opened from the inside. Hunter recoiled in shock at the sight of the woman who held it open for them. Tall, graceful with dark brown hair and an ageless beauty. Beverley Murphy.

"Bev?" He gasped.

Bev turned her eyes to the floor, looking so meek compared to the fierce, but friendly mum they'd visited. The older woman muttered her excuses and left, sparing Hunter a single glance. Hunter was left with the idea that she was somehow angry, or perhaps just disappointed with him.

The door closed, shutting Bev from sight as she hurried down the corridor. Back in the room, Hunter noticed the soft-looking chairs, a roaring fire and a table with breakfast on. Three things that hypnotised him after a cold, uncomfortable night.

"I have brought Astley, ma'am." The lead witch said with a note of pride, and Hunter had the impression that it was all she could do not to bow or curtsy to the Shadow Witch.

Sophie was sitting close to the fire and turned her head to look at the group. "Bring him here."

Hunter was (unnecessarily) shoved towards Sophie. Sophie looked him over with those cold, analytical eyes of hers.

"You may go," she said, dismissing the others.

The witches hesitated, and again it was the female witch that spoke, but hesitantly, as though she feared offending Sophie, or revealing some ignorance.

"Please, ma'am - he - surely it is safer for us to stay."

Sophie glared at the witch, an aura of power rising threateningly. "I can manage Astley. Now go."

The witch frowned, unconvinced, but obediently left the room, with her heavies in tow.

The Shadow Witch, or Sophie, which should she now be known by? She waited for the other witches to leave then set her eyes solidly on Hunter, her expression lightening with a familiarity that seemed sinful now.

"You look terrible," she said with a frown, looking at the bruises and half-healed cuts that decorated any skin on show.

"I ran into a few of your new friends at the prison," Hunter answered irritably.

"I'd hardly call them friends. As for new - I have known them a lot longer than I've known you."

"Saw your mother outside. Is she part of your little army too?" Hunter spat bitterly.

"My mother is here of her own free will. She had every right to be a part of this. And before you ask, yes, she is a witch, although her powers were bound before she was born. Now, will you join me for breakfast - a cup of coffee at least?" Sophie asked, as though everything were normal.

"It's kind of difficult to hold a cup behind my back," Hunter replied pointedly.

"Oh, of course." She rose from her seat in a graceful movement, stepping next to him at once.

Tired as he was, Hunter forced himself to remember that this was the Shadow Witch as he breathed in that familiar, enticing scent. There was a faint click and the cuffs fell away from his wrists.

"I'm sorry, but I'm sure you understand, it's for my colleagues' safety," Sophie said gently, then returned to her seat with a smile.

"One question," Hunter said, his voice rough.

"Just one?"

"For now."

Sophie watched him carefully. "Ok then. Why don't you sit down?"

Hunter sat slowly, hating the soft, comfy seat and having an odd déjà vu of when Sophie had first come to Astley Manor seeking his help. "Answer me truthfully, is Sophie, my Sophie, the Shadow Witch?"

She sighed. "Your Sophie is, and always has been, the Shadow Witch."

Hunter took a deep breath, and sat silently.

Sophie watched him with cool curiosity. "Help yourself to coffee and toast - if you're in the mood for something else, I'm sure I can magic it up."

Hunter ignored her dry humour. He looked suspiciously at the pot of coffee, but didn't take any, wary of poison and potions. He turned his gaze back to Sophie, she was still cold, beautiful, intelligent - but everything had changed. She was now the enemy. The Shadow Witch, against whom they all fought. The woman responsible for plunging the world into chaos and darkness.

"Come now, Hunter," Sophie said bitterly. "You're not going to sulk, are you?"

"Why?"

"Why what?"

Hunter gazed unflinchingly at the young woman. "Everything. Why did you pretend to be a hunter? Why am I here? Why haven't you killed me yet?"

And more, unspoken questions hung tangibly in the air, why did you get so close, was it all a pretence?

177

"Everything is a lot to tell, Hunter, you've already accused me of gloating, why should I indulge you?" Sophie sat, quite unperturbed, casually continuing with her breakfast.

"Back in Italy, I saved you from witches. Was that planned?" Hunter persevered.

Sophie seemed to be measuring him up, then suddenly smiled more openly than Hunter had ever seen. "You really want to know, to hear every devious detail?"

"Tell me."

"Ok. I wanted to learn from my natural enemies, the best way I possibly could. So I planned a little sacrifice with me as the innocent victim, then I would use my ample negotiating skills to become a witch-hunter - what better way to learn about the MMC than to be part of it.

"I chose to stage it in Venice, back in the 'old country' one could say, it would all be safer and easier to pull in an Italian witch-hunter, away from my roots. Which is where you messed things up." Her eyes flicked up on him, she looked half-amused, half-angry. "You, of all witch-hunters, Astley, so closely tied to my family. You turned up and were my hero, slaying the evil witches and rescuing me from certain death. I was so angry that I could have killed you there and then, and blown everything we'd worked towards."

"So what, you allowed other witches to get killed to make the scene more believable?" Hunter asked, disgusted.

"You really think me that cruel, that ambitious as to sacrifice my own kin?" Sophie asked with a soft shake of her head. "No. Although we were not short of volunteers. The male you killed was a bewitched wiccan, there for you to get your blood quota. The two females were witches, under orders to make sure it all ran smoothly and then to surrender. After all, they knew they'd be free to fight again."

Hunter was suddenly hit with an array of memory - his own research into a wiccan found with witches, the arson attack, Charlotte commenting on the increase in bound witches... they all knew they would get released and restored.

"What, should I applaud you for your ingenuity?" Hunter asked bitterly, feeling a wave of nausea and shame. He'd fallen for it, every part. He'd killed a human - a wiccan albeit, but human all the same. He felt sick.

"No," Sophie mused. "But I would like to thank you, for pulling strings with the Council and getting me a place as a 1st gen."

"Brian. You killed him." It wasn't a question, the truth was hovering there in front of Hunter.

Sophie shrugged, "It was very frustrating. For one exciting moment I thought you'd take me on - I would have the chance to fool the best there was, it was thrilling. But perhaps it was best that I went to Brian first, his senses were so unevolved compared to yours, I didn't have to worry about slipping up as much.

"He taught me a lot, even though he was a condescending sexist bastard. I often struggled to stay calm when he treated me as less than nothing - I, the greatest witch for almost a century. But I was willing to put up with it.

179

"Then I found out that Brian was doing work and research on the side, he'd made links with the unusual events that we had not completely covered. He was getting too close and needed removing, along with all his work. I have a certain skill for pure destruction, as you saw at his house. I had to make sure that everything was eradicated, I didn't want the MMC knowing that a Shadow had risen. Not until I was ready."

Hunter couldn't help but smile ruefully, good old Brian, the grumpy old sod would've been pleased to be so inconvenient. "You slipped up, we got the info and discovered the return of the Shadow Witch."

She nodded in fair agreement, but her smile didn't fade. "Yes, and thank you again, this time for taking me in. I admit that at first I wanted to destroy all the information, but that would draw unnecessary attention. So instead I spent the next week, on your orders, searching for anything important in the notes and reports, then secretly removing anything that was too obvious. It was rather interesting to learn about what I was from a witch-hunter's perspective."

"We still found out though." Hunter argued, remembering vividly the night after Brian's memorial service.

"I underestimated you," Sophie admitted. "But it didn't matter in the end, you learnt nothing that would endanger me and your MMC refused to act. In fact it worked out better than I could have ever dreamt - I got to see what protection and weapons you had to use against me. It was pitiful."

"Then let me guess, you left as soon as possible and struck and now you've won," Hunter said bitterly, not wanting to hear more of her gloating confessions, yet desperate for answers.

"As soon as possible," Sophie repeated under her breath with a hint of regret that surprised Hunter.

"So, now you've revealed all your evil doings, are you going to cackle madly and kill me?"

"Evil?" Sophie asked, almost sadly. "Do you really think me evil? You think I've done this to hurt you? I have done what is right for my kind - freeing them from persecution by you and your bloodthirsty Council. You - you demand that we witches do not live by our nature, that we should be vilified because we are something more than you. What gives you and the MMC the right to impose morals and judgement on what you don't understand?"

Hunter didn't meet her eye, he didn't want to get into a moral debate, especially with someone that presented their facts so civilly.

"You didn't answer my question," he reminded her.

Sophie hesitated. "They want you dead. The others, the witches' council. They fear that I grew too close to you and they want proof that I can kill the best the witch-hunters have. They argue that your death will be the ultimate blow for the remnants of the MMC and will further boost our morale and power."

She paused, and when she spoke again it was with carefully restrained anger, her hazel eyes blazing. "And how I long to kill you Astley. How I have cursed you every day of my life for what your family took from the witchkind, from me."

Again, hesitation. Sophie shrugged, the anger fading quickly as she fell back into her cushioned chair. "But I'm not going to kill you. Instead I'm going to offer you something. To join the witches, instead of fighting them. Together we can create a greatness that will eclipse everything that has gone before. We will build the world to our standard. You would be a ruler, answering to no one - except me of course."

Hunter sat in a state of shock. He definitely hadn't been expecting that. To never have to await MMC approval again, to switch to the winning side, to have Sophie with him. It was incredibly tempting. His mouth was dry as he responded.

"Ah, no, I'm going to turn you down because I don't want to sell my soul. Besides, I don't think your witchy pals would agree to a witch-hunter in their ranks, especially when you say they're all so keen to see me dead."

Sophie smiled at his goading reply, which was a rather disconcerting reaction.

"Have you ever heard of the Benandanti?" She suddenly asked.

Hunter scowled, but finally agreed to reply. "No."

"Let me tell you a little story."

"Another one?" Hunter snorted.

Sophie ignored him and started to speak again. "In Friuli, Italy, there was a small peasant group called the Benandanti. They lived simply enough, with one special feature, they protected themselves and those around them from witches, and had been doing so for centuries. This was a very elite group, one couldn't just join the Benandanti, one had to be born into the clan.

182

They were special, bred to repel witches; they were stronger, faster, could even detect magic being used. They could travel far distances in a blink, they could change the world around them to chase off, or even destroy witches.

"They lived peaceful little lives with surrounding villages. But they were discovered by witch-hunters and, in self-reflection saw that they had become what they most feared. Witches."

Hunter frowned, an uneasy feeling about where this was heading.

"Don't you see? Did you never wonder what the witch-hunter generations were leading to? What you are, a 7th gen?" Sophie asked, excited now, leaning forward with her eyes glittering. "Just think of the possibilities."

Hunter let the flickering fire in the grate distract him, watching the sparks from the logs. Stronger, faster. He knew that he was gifted - an unheard of 7th gen. No one knew what he was capable of. But having magic?

"Nice theory. But I think you're a couple of generations early. I'm no witch."

"Have you ever tried?" Sophie questioned. "It didn't come easily to me when my powers were first awoken. It took months to gain control. And I know it is you, I have seen you use magic with my own eyes."

This made Hunter pay attention. "What? I've never-"

"Hallowe'en." Sophie interrupted. "At the church. I had the key from Charlotte and every piece of information I needed, so pulled in our best witches to finish off you and James - you had both outlived your uses. Then I felt something I didn't understand, a huge build-up of magic that I didn't recognise. And such a release to rival even my own. Then I saw amongst the rubble and bodies you, standing alone and untouched with an aura of magic that outclassed so many."

Hallowe'en. Hunter had tried not to think about it, it was too painful. But it all came rushing back with amazing clarity. Charlotte lying there as though asleep, then out of the silence James alerting him to the witches. There had been so many, by all logic he should have been killed that night. But Hunter had been so distraught that at the time he had acted without thinking. Afterwards he had not thought about it, the eerie lack of magic as the church blew apart. He and James had assumed that it was the work of the Shadow Witch.

"You're lying."

"No Hunter, I'm not," Sophie replied softly.

"Do the others know this?"

"No." Sophie admitted. "They think you're just a normal witch-hunter that I like to toy with. Please, Hunter, this is the only way – it's either live like a god with me, or be killed by the others."

Hunter watched her carefully, she wasn't threatening him, it was more of a warning. But what did she care if he lived or died, after all he was just a plaything.

"And what about James?"

"What about him?" Sophie said impatiently, not wanting to get off topic. "His fate was sealed when he came here, I couldn't save him if I wanted to. Besides, he's not important, you are."

Hunter looked at her with disbelief. How could he ever have thought he could love her. This amoral women that had murdered Brian, Charlotte, and would throw away James' life so easily.

"Promise you'll think on it. Just remember that I can only keep you safe for a day at the most."

Sophie looked away to the door and Hunter felt a ripple of magic in the air, he tensed, but nothing happened.

"Relax, I've just called the others. They'll take you back to your room unharmed," Sophie said, standing up.

Hunter heard the click of the door handle and he sprang from his seat. Unarmed and outnumbered, this was still his best chance.

As though reading his desperate thoughts Sophie rushed forward and grabbed him, with a surprising force she turned him towards her and suddenly kissed him.

Along with her familiar lips and warm breath, something passed to Hunter. He staggered away, his limbs suddenly leaden and shaking. He looked up to Sophie, her face swimming.

"For your own good, Astley." She said quietly.

And then he blacked out.

Twenty-two

When Hunter came to, he was lying on a hard wooden floor. He felt very odd, the aching pain from his last injuries felt distant, like they didn't belong to him. He groaned slightly from a pounding headache - he could feel that.

"Hunter? You awake?"

Hunter opened his eyes a fraction to see the blurry image of James hovering over him.

"Yeah," he grunted.

"Thank god. When they brought you in, I thought - but it doesn't matter now."

Hunter fully opened his eyes and his gaze returned to its usual sharpness. Daylight poured in through the one sealed window. "How long have I been out?"

"A few hours." James replied, helping him to sit up.

Hunter recoiled. "Jesus, what happened?"

James winced. His eyes were dark and puffy, promising some stunning bruises, dry blood spotted beneath a newly broken nose, and from the way he held himself it looked like a cracked rib or two.

"The witches. They've been forbidden from using any magic on us, so they delighted in practising more mortal forms of violence. Don't worry, it looks worse than it is." James tried to take a deep breath, but grunted with pain. "Actually, scratch that."

He stood, collecting himself for a few minutes. Hunter could only imagine how the witches had taken it all out on poor James while he was away being breakfasted by their boss.

"Come on then, tell us everything. It'll help distract from the pain," James said, half hopeful.

Hunter repeated everything Sophie had revealed, interrupted frequently by James' questions which he did his best to answer.

James gave a low whistle after he'd finished. "You know, if we get out of this alive, we'll never live this down. The Shadow Witch living under our noses the whole time."

Hunter could only give a twisted smile in agreement, he was feeling guilty over the whole affair.

"Did Sophie say why we're here? I mean, they haven't killed us yet."

Oh dear. Hunter didn't want to mention this to anyone, if it was true, the MMC would have to treat him as a witch; or he'd have to do the decent thing and end his own life - neither were appealing. But telling James was different, surely. He could trust years of friendship.

"Have you heard of the Benandanti?"

"Sure, an Italian pagan group of anti-witches that developed powers of their own and were ultimately prosecuted for it. Why?" James reeled off, making Hunter just a little jealous of his infinite knowledge.

"Sophie thinks I might be one. Or something similar." Hunter confessed.

That silenced James. Hunter didn't underestimate James' intelligence he'd probably figured out everything Hunter hadn't said.

*****

The witches brought food and drink for them that evening, and although wary, they were too hungry and thirsty to care about poison.

That night they took shifts again keeping watch. The first few hours passed by without incidence, and Hunter nudged James awake, stifling a yawn as he did so. He waited for his friend to be entirely conscious before allowing himself to drift off. Before he had a chance to sleep though, James grabbed his arm painfully tight.

Reopening his eyes, Hunter saw across the room the light from the bulb was fading, darkness and shadow forming.

"Sophie?" Hunter tried to call, but his voice came out a whisper.

A figure stepped out of the shadows, tall and gracefully slender with long brown hair and a beautiful but older face than they were expecting.

"Bev?"

The two guys sat stunned, and more than a tad confused.

She motioned for them to be quiet, while pulling a large bag off her back.

"I've come to get you out of here," she whispered.

"But... how? Sophie sealed this place, only she can undo it." Hunter whispered back.

Bev frowned in a familiar way. "I am her mother and I know a few tricks. I've borrowed her powers, Sophie is drugged and none the wiser."

So a loving, caring mother, Hunter thought, but had the wisdom to say none of it aloud.

"But how?" He repeated. "And why should we trust you?"

"Why should you trust me? How many other witches are here offering to help you escape?" Bev asked hurriedly. "As for how, Sara Murray was my grandmother. I could have been the next Shadow Witch, but I didn't want it. Yet I can siphon off a little of my daughter's powers now. I may only be able to do this once, though."

Sara Murray, the previous Shadow Witch that Old George had killed in the 1940s.

"Sara Murray didn't have kids," James whispered.

"She did," Bev replied. "But when she became the Shadow Witch she knew her daughter, my mother, wouldn't be safe. So she bound her powers, and had her adopted, then destroyed all evidence of her existence. Please understand Sara was a good woman who didn't deserve to be a tool of evil. Who knows what good could have come from her. But Astley killed her and planted a seed of hatred and revenge in the heart of every witch. I tried to protect Sophie from it all, but she took it to heart, carried the promise of revenge as her own burden."

"Why are you telling us all this now?" Hunter asked.

189

Bev looked away from them and sighed. "I want you to understand why Sophie seems - she has her reasons. But we must be quick."

"We're unarmed and locked up," James hissed.

Bev knelt down and opened the bag. She pulled out two hunting shotguns and two kitchen knives. "The best I could do, I'm sorry. Now, I think I can manage to get you into the grounds."

With an intense look of concentration, the thick shadow rippled along the wall to head height. Without notice, she grabbed them both by the arm and stepped into the darkness.

Again, Hunter felt surrounded by warm nothingness. But it didn't last long. The cold night air hit him hard, he couldn't help but shiver. The night sky was cloudy, and it was hard to see anything. He turned round and only a couple of hundred yards behind him was the shadow of a huge house, with light pouring out of windows.

"I have done what I can," Bev suddenly said. "I have to go back."

"Wait, come with us." Hunter argued, surprising himself with the offer. "There's so much more you could tell us. And to be honest we could do with the help."

Bev didn't reply immediately, but stared back at the house with shining eyes. "Sophie is my daughter. Whatever happens, I have to stand by her. She needs me, or at least she soon will."

If either of the men understood this, they didn't say anything.

"Well, thank you." James finally said awkwardly. "We owe you our lives."

"You owe me nothing." Bev replied. "I didn't do it for you, I did it for Sophie."

Bev turned to a frowning Hunter. "If you were killed, it would destroy her. And she could never kill you herself, for two reasons. Mainly because - as much as she denies it - she loves you, irrevocably. Ah, I must go before they miss me."

"Wait," Hunter said, reaching out. "You said two reasons. What's the second?"

Bev's eyes met his in the dark. "She is pregnant with your child."

And she was gone.

Twenty-three

The two men ran into the night, Hunter leading with his sharper sight. They had no idea where they were or where they were heading, only running to get away from that house of witches.

Ahead of them lay only darkness. It was eerie to see the English countryside without the punctuation of lights from roads or villages. But they just kept going, hoping to stumble on some form of civilisation.

Eventually they hit tarmac and followed the road to a sleeping town. The houses sat in absolute shadow, and as they walked past, a couple of dogs stirred and barked, but no one came out to see two men armed with guns and knives walking down the nighttime street.

Hunter looked at the cars parked along the roadside. "Can you get one of these running?"

James got closer so his weaker eyes could see the shiny new BMW. "No. But... trust me on this. Come on."

Without explaining himself, James set off down the street, stopping to look at each car. Then, as though making his mind up, he raised his gun and used is to bash in the driver's window. There was a loud shatter of glass.

Hunter frowned at James' choice. An M-reg rustbucket of a Fiesta. A worrying option, because it was essential for them to make it all the way home, however far that might be. "Do you think this one ever worked?"

James used his sleeve to get the worst of the glass off the driver's seat. "Look, I had a lot of time to think when they treated me as a punchbag, at least, thinking helped distract me. I have a theory about their little powercut."

He broke off, pulling out his knife and busying himself under the steering wheel. He suddenly swore and pulled back, sucking his freshly bleeding hand.

"Not the best tool for the job," he admitted. "Anyway, as I was sayin'. The lights and the phone went dead. But not all technology was knocked out - our torches worked, your mobile phone battery still worked, you just didn't have any signal. Hey - you still got your phone?"

Hunter frowned, but rather than try to make sense of James he reached into his pocket. Miraculously his phone was still there.

"Cool, flick up the screen so I can get some light an' see what I'm doing."

Hunter did as directed and held his glowing phone near the dangling wires. James tinkered for a minute and was rewarded by guttural choking, followed by the small engine rumbling to life.

"Well done, now shift over." Hunter said, pushing James over to the passenger seat. He frowned at the wheel, never having driven such a wreck. "But James, you didn't give your theory."

James clipped on his seat belt as Hunter pulled away, the old engine roaring and lights showing up an empty country road.

"Theory? Oh yeah, well they knocked out all the big and complex stuff - even down to your watch. So anything that requires power or radio signal. But very simple technology with its own power source wasn't affected."

"Which is why you wanted the old car?" Hunter said slowly, catching on.

"Yes, less electronics that could go wrong." James replied with a yawn.

*****

As they rattled along empty roads the wind whipped in through the broken window, freezing Hunter to his seat, but keeping him bloody awake. Next to him, James snored lightly. Hunter felt so guilty about what he'd gone through, that he barely felt jealous of him getting some sleep.

He wouldn't have been able to sleep anyway. His body clock told him it was around five or six o'clock in the morning, the world was still dark and silent.

In his mind he lived and relived everything from the moment he'd met Sophie, seeing it all in a new light. She'd played them all perfectly, made Hunter believe that he…

He didn't know when he fell in love with her, it had happened so quickly, yet the realisation had taken weeks to crawl up to him. He remembered her mother, Bev, warning him off - he had assumed she was being an overly protective mum, not trying to save him from - from this. But she had already been too late, he had already been falling under Sophie's spell.

He grimaced at his private thought's choice of word.

Had Sophie cast a spell he hadn't felt? Or slipped a love potion in the many coffees she had brought him? All to blind him from what she was really up to.

'As much as she denies it - she loves you irrevocably.' Bev's words rang again in his ears. He could only hope it was true, that she would never kill him because she loved him.

But... what about her, would he be able to kill her?

Of course, the voice of reason screamed, she was the Shadow Witch and needed to be destroyed. But when Hunter imagined himself standing in front of Sophie and pulling the trigger-

He leant forward, trying to let the road drive out the image. It was only an enchantment, it would wear off. He'd be able to stop thinking about her, get back to normal.

It wasn't long before his spinning thoughts came inevitably to the very disturbing idea that he could be a witch. Here, alone in the dark (a snoring James didn't count), it seemed scarily possible. Each generation of witch-hunter took them further away from their human roots. Why shouldn't the next step be magic.

Hunter sighed, he hadn't asked for it and didn't want it. But if he was entirely honest with himself, if it turned out that he was strong enough to oppose the Shadow Witch it could only help. Like the anti-witch Benandanti. Only one problem, really, he'd never intentionally used magic and he'd seen how skilled Sophie was.

Hunter leant closer to the windscreen, concentrating on keeping up a decent speed in the old Fiesta as he navigated amongst the cars that had been abandoned by their owners. They must have been travelling at the time of the hit, there were signs of collisions as drivers lost control as their trusty vehicles gave up. Hunter wondered how many had been hurt, and his fears were raised as something caught his eye. He squinted into the dark, not sure what he was seeing. The car's headlights picked up increasingly large chunks of debris across the abandoned motorway.

Hunter pulled up on the side of the road and nudged James awake, before climbing out of the car. In front of them the tarmac was ripped up and the grass bank was a churned mess of mud and metal. Hunter clambered up the short bank with James stumbling behind him. The remnants of an aeroplane crash landed.

"Hunter..." James caught up with him. "Hunter come on, there's nothing we can do."

Hunter ignored him and ran over to the fallen craft, he paused at one of the gaping holes, then ducked inside. He called out, but there was no response. As his eyes adapted to the near-pitch darkness inside, Hunter saw that the plane was empty.

"Is there anyone there?" James asked, standing in the broken gap.

Hunter made his way back out of the plane, taking a deep breath. "No. Whether they survived or not, they've already been moved. But then it has been 34 hours since the hit."

Hunter shuddered and walked slowly back to the car, the little old Fiesta was still running with lights on and doors thrown wide at the bottom of the small slope.

The two friends got back in and set off once more, both silenced by what they'd seen. Both of them could only guess at the extent of the damage done.

*****

There was the thin grey light of a late winter's dawn as they finally turned out of the village of Little Hanting and onto the Astley estate. Right on cue, James groaned and woke up.

"Home?" He muttered.

"Yes, two minutes," Hunter replied shortly, starting to feel tired again as the familiar ground flicked by.

They were driving straight up towards the Manor when a man stepped into their headlights, blocking the way. He waved at them to stop. More commanding was the gun he aimed at the windscreen.

"Who goes there?" The man shouted as the car stopped.

Hunter leaned out, "Hunter Astley, 7th gen; and James Bennett, 1st gen."

The witch-hunter didn't move or lower his weapon. "Do you have proof of identity?"

"Proof?" Hunter gasped, not in the mood for this. "Look, this is my bloody house, so if you don't mind shifting."

197

The witch-hunter looked uncertain, but a second armed figure moved in the darkness to their right. He began to walk warily towards them, then stopped. "Mr Astley? You're back. Let him pass, Dan."

The first man moved aside and Hunter got the rattling vehicle down the remaining short length of drive to the front of the Manor. The Fiesta stuttered to a rolling stop as the engine packed in with perfect timing.

Hunter and James went into the wonderfully familiar Manor, and were immediately surrounded by witch-hunters.

"Mr Astley, thank god. We feared the worst when we lost contact." Anthony Marks, the 5th gen that had been in charge in their absence now stepped forward.

The worst? Yes, the worst had happened, Hunter thought sleepily. His bed was upstairs, warm and comfortable.

"Communications have been down for two days, we've been struggling to track down other witch-hunters, trying to re-establish links with police and army forces."

"Yes, the Shadow Witch knocked out everything technological. James'll explain later," Hunter said, struggling to pay attention. "Right now, we have to prepare for an attack. The Shadow Witch is coming. As soon as she finds out that we've escaped she'll know where to find us. She could be here at any moment, so we don't have time to lose."

"But the Manor is safe against her."

Hunter nodded. "Even if it is, it won't stop her coming as close as possible and forcing us to fight - I

198

think we may have managed to piss her off. Little Hanting. The village, it needs evacuating. Get the villagers as far away as possible, or get them in here if there's room, I don't care."

The surrounding witch-hunters stood there looking far too gormless for Hunter's liking. "Well, go!"

Hunter turned to James who, although still looking a bruised mess, was keen and wide-awake. "I'm going to lie down. Wake me when - when it's time."

Twenty-four

Hunter felt like he'd only closed his eyes for ten minutes when he was suddenly shaken awake. His eyes snapped open and he bolted upright. Sitting on his bed was a familiar figure.

"James?" How long have I slept?"

"Um, dunno, 'bout ten minutes." He replied distractedly.

Hunter groaned, but pulled back his covers and started looking for his shoes. "Sophie's here already? I had hoped we'd have more time to prepare."

"What? No, she's not here yet." James replied.

"Then what...?" Hunter frowned at his friend, tempted to push him off the bed, roll over and go back to sleep. "James, you are a pain in the arse. What is this about then?"

James looked down at a book he held in his hands. When he spoke it was in a conspiring whisper. "The Benandanti. I knew I'd seen info on them in the library, so I went t'find it."

Hunter sighed, but paid attention, his nerves sparking inside him. "Anything useful?"

"Depends," James answered. "I've only flicked through, but it does describe some of their, ah, abilities. Eye witness accounts of Benandanti standing in front of witches: a feeling of a cushioning atmosphere that blocked all use of magic, forcing witches to fight by mortal means."

Now that did sound promising, but Hunter still frowned. "If, if I'm capable of that, would it apply against a Shadow Witch - magic without limits? And does it say how it's done?"

James paused, scanning through the marked pages. Eventually he shrugged. "No, no mention on how. You'll have to work that out alone. As for bein' up against a Shadow, I doubt the Benandanti ever met one."

Hunter stared at the book unseeingly. "Do you think this is how Sophie worked it out?"

"Probably. She had open access to the Astley collection and library," James replied honestly, sharing a portion of the guilt and shame.

"I think we can assume that, even with my questionable abilities, Sophie will be prepared. She'll bring a small army of witches."

James didn't interrupt, but did wonder how Hunter could sound so sure.

"An army of witches." Hunter repeated quietly. "And we have what, fifty witch-hunters?"

"Forty-three," James corrected.

A pitiful number, sure to be crushed. They personally seen thirty witches just in that house.

Hunter didn't doubt that Sophie could double or triple that within hours. Hopefully she'll be impatient and come with only a handful of witches, rather than patiently mustering more.

"Why don't we build our own army?" James suddenly asked.

"What, with forty-three witch-hunters? Or are you suggesting that the villagers of Little Hanting join in?"

James ignored his sarcasm. "No, I mean the actual army. They've gotta be on alert after the comms went down. If we get some troops here we'll be winning on numbers."

"James!" Hunter cut into his enthusiasm. "First of all, they aren't witch-hunters."

"But they are trained," James argued.

"And numbers might not help against a Shadow," Hunter persevered.

"But they'll help, 'specially if you knock out the magic."

"And the closest base is nearly two hours away. Even if someone set off now, by the time the troops were kitted and mobilised, they couldn't get back here for what, five hours. It could be too late."

James shook his head, opening his book again. "Look, the Benandanti could travel in the blink of an eye. You could go tell them. Even if you can't transport them with you, it'll cut two hours off the time."

"James, I am not Benandanti!" Hunter argued. Yes, things would all work out if he did have all these powers, but all he felt was bloody useless at this point.

"Just try, what's the harm?"

The harm? He could be accused of witchcraft and cast out by the witch-hunters when they needed him most.

"Even if I can, it might not be soon enough. What if she attacks while I'm away?"

"Then you will survive to fight again and find a way to destroy the Shadow Witch," James answered seriously. "Hunter, try, you're our only hope."

"I don't know how," Hunter continued to argue.

"Concentrate, I guess," James said encouragingly. "Ah, if it works, I'll keep an eye on the others. I think its best that they don't know 'bout this til necessary."

Hunter stood up and instinctively closed his eyes. Feeling rather stupid he twisted his mind, trying to feel something, tingly, or warm and smothered like the Shadow.

"This is never going to work." He muttered, opening his eyes.

"Just keep concentrating." James suggested. "Picture yourself on base."

Hunter took a deep breath and closed his eyes again. He remembered visiting the base when he'd first joined the MMC, he'd been to see the general, an open-minded, trustworthy man who'd been made aware of the witch threat and occasionally passed on witch-sightings and helped with some of the cover-ups.

Hunter could see clearly the general's office, with the desk and walls decorated with photos and certificates. It all seemed out of reach.

"I feel stupid." He muttered.

There was a faint click and a man's voice came from behind him.

"Raise your hands and turn slowly to face me."

Hunter's eyes flew open, instead of his navy bedroom there were cream walls. He lifted his hands and span quickly to see the familiar office.

There was the crack of a pistol as the man fired at his hasty movements. Hunter's eyes widened with fear and his heart leapt... but nothing hit him. He looked down, confused. A shining bullet hovered just inches from his chest. Stopped dead.

"Huh. That's useful." Hunter reached out to touch it. His finger brushed the metal, before he swore and snapped his hand back from the heat. Hunter frowned and stared at the little thing, then it dropped onto the floor.

Hunter looked up. There was a shocked middle-aged man standing behind a desk, holding a gun with impressive steadiness. It had been a few years, but he was still recognisable.

"General Hayworth." Hunter stepped towards him, hesitating as he realised that he was barefoot. Bother, next time he'd have to remember to be fully dressed before attempting transporting himself.

"Sir, my name's Hunter Astley, from the Malleus Maleficarum Council. We met a few years ago."

"Astley? Astley, yes I remember." The general glanced down at his bare feet with a frown. "We thought only witches appeared out of nowhere."

The general half-shrugged and lowered his gun, obviously thinking he'd given enough explanation for having fired at the sudden appearance of a person in his office.

"It's a long story," Hunter admitted. "But I don't have time to explain everything. We need your help. We know where the Shadow Witch will strike next, we just need an army to face her."

The door of the office suddenly opened and a younger man burst in. He stopped, staring at the General and witch-hunter. "General, I, ah, heard a gunshot."

"It's nothing, Dawkins, return to your post," General Hayworth replied calmly.

The young man, obedient but confused, backed out of the office, closing the door behind him.

"Sit down, Astley." The general said, motioning to a chair in front of his desk. "As I was saying to Marks before the phones went down, the army doesn't take orders from your MMC. In times of chaos we have to follow the proper channels, but-"

"But we don't have time to follow the proper channels," Hunter interrupted with frustration. "The Shadow Witch could attack at any time."

"Will you let me finish, Mr Astley?" The General said patiently. "But, I understand that things have changed. Those that wrote the rules could not have predicted this. I also understand that the MMC may well know best. Yet my men are not trained to fight witches."

"You can't choose your enemies," Hunter reasoned.

"No, but we are better defending than fighting," The general mused. "Your Council does know best, I suppose. We will rally to your aid."

General Hayworth walked over to the door and opened it. "Sergeant!"

205

Dawkins reappeared obediently. "Yes, General?"

"I want the men armed and ready to leave in thirty minutes. Then return here."

Dawkins blinked with surprise. "Yes General."

The sergeant disappeared down the corridor to pass on the order.

"Thank you, General," Hunter said as the general closed the door and returned to his seat.

"Don't thank me yet," he replied. "You have half an hour to explain this to me."

Twenty-five

Hunter decided that relaying his story was the least he could do for this good man. Hunter went over a lot, but not everything, he left out most of his mistakes, aware as he did so that he was leaving gaping holes in his story.

The General just sat there, building up a better understanding of their enemy. He raised a brow whenever he felt that Hunter was being evasive or less than honest, but said nothing until he'd finished.

"I agree that we need to get to Little Hanting as soon as possible. That travel 'in a blink' thing you did, can you take others?"

"I - I don't know." Hunter replied truthfully. "I haven't really had time to work it out."

The General nodded and stood up, going to his office door once more. "Dawkins!"

The mild young man popped in for the third time.

"Yes General?"

"I'm going to inspect the troops, Dawkins. You are going to help Mr Astley with a little experiment." He turned to Hunter. "Astley, I want a definite answer in fifteen minutes."

General Hayworth exited the office, leaving Hunter with a now very pale Dawkins.

"Experiment?" The sergeant asked weakly.

Hunter hesitated. He could try explaining it to the fellow, but he'd be likelier to scare him rather than reassure him. The idea of taking another person along brought up a lot of questions for Hunter. What if it didn't work? Or worse, what if it only partially worked and half of poor Dawkins got left behind?

"Just... stand still and bear with me." Hunter suggested, shutting out his worries.

Hunter reached out and held the sergeant's arm tightly. He shut his eyes and pictured home. He took a deep breath and opened his eyes.

Damn, still the office. Dawkins stood tense and still beside him.

Hunter frowned, concentrate, concentrate. Home, his room with the oak panelling, the cream and navy sheets and curtains, the table with the-

Hunter felt Dawkins snatch away from him and feared the worst. His eyes snapped open. The first thing he saw was his bedroom; the second was a very whole and very pale Dawkins.

"Yes!" Hunter shouted. Finally something had gone right.

"How do you feel? All in one piece? Dizzy?" Hunter asked the sergeant rapidly.

Dawkins gazed about him open-mouthed and wide-eyed. "What was...? Ah, yes sir, fine sir. A little dizzy I guess."

"Great." Hunter replied. "Ok, I've got to get back to General Hayworth, you might as well stay here. Go downstairs, find someone called James Bennett. Tell him Hunter is going to bring the army."

Hunter broke off. He didn't know how many men would be coming, but no part of his Manor would hold even a hundred, he'd struggle to get even fifty into any room.

"Tell James they'll be in Little Hanting's church hall within the hour."

Hunter was getting excited now. Death and war beckoned to them, but now they had a chance. He stood tall and closed his eyes to go back to the General's office, then broke off.

"Shoes, shoes…" He pulled them out from under his bed and hopped about as he pulled them on. He grabbed his coat and closed his eyes.

When he opened them he was in General Hayworth's office. This blinking thing was getting easier. Hunter felt hope burn bright in his chest as he left the office to find the General.

Outside, a hundred soldiers stood, kitted and ready, silent and waiting. Hunter could see a single figure moving up and down the ranks, the general inspecting the troops.

Hunter ran up, aware of the many eyes that followed him.

General Hayworth took one look at him. "So you were successful?"

Hunter nodded, then couldn't help but smile. He was bristling with the excitement and opportunity of this new ability.

"Well, let's get this over with." The general said. "How do you suggest we go about this? It'll take a while to go one at a time. Can you take several?"

Hunter, buoyed up by recent success was thinking of something a little more effective. "I have an idea. Can we use a wall?"

Without explaining himself, Hunter turned to the nearest building and went up to the side wall that stretched about 10 metres wide. The Shadow Witch had done it with shadows, why shouldn't he be able to do it with what was on hand.

"I figure that if I create and maintain a link you should all be able to, well, to march on through." Hunter tried to sound convincing.

General Hayworth frowned, but sighed. The General was out of his depth where magic was concerned, he'd go along with almost anything at this point. After all, what did they have to lose.

"Very well." He turned to his troops. "Fall in, four abreast. Forward march."

There was the co-ordinated movement of well-trained men. The General halted them in front of the building.

"When you're ready, Astley."

Hunter tried to ignore how very pale and dubious the first four men at the front of the column looked, and placed his hand on the cold brick. Closing his eyes he did his best to picture the old church hall, without going there himself. Ready, he nodded.

On command the first four stepped and - slammed into the wall. Hunter opened his eyes as about him soldiers laughed with a note of panic.

210

"Wait, wait, I've got it now, I promise," Hunter said, concentrating so hard it was difficult to get the words out.

The General ordered his men to go again, which they did gingerly, reaching out and finding their hands passing through the solid wall. This caused as much subdued panic as before, but soon the men marched through under the stern eye of their General.

Gradually the court cleared as the troops disappeared. Hunter was sweating with the exertion of keeping the link, he had no idea it would be so hard to concentrate for so long. As the last soldier stepped through, Hunter broke off from the wall and bent over at the knee, his heart pounding and breath panting, a wave of exhaustion came over him as though he'd just ran a bloody marathon. He vaguely thought that he should have made them all drive instead.

"Buck up, Astley," came the general's voice. "You're not done just yet."

Hunter took a deep breath and stood up straight. He dutifully took hold of General Hayworth's arm. One more trip, he'd manage it, he'd have to.

When he opened his eyes, Hunter was surrounded by soldiers beneath the dusty roof of the old village hall. Next to him, General Hayworth looked about business-like, apparently unfazed by the magical journey.

They'd only been there a minute when Sergeant Dawkins and Anthony Marks pushed their way towards them. Hunter didn't like the look on Marks' face, and guessed what was coming. But any

211

unpleasantness was put off by the necessary introductions and briefings.

"… squads are placed beyond Astley Manor, we were just dividing the rest to place about the village," Dawkins reeled off, obviously recovered from his earlier shock.

"We can't thank you enough, General," Marks said.

"We're all on the same side, Mr Marks," General Hayworth replied, brushing aside his thanks. They could be grateful when, and if, they won.

Marks nodded, then finally turned to Hunter. "A word please, Mr Astley."

Oh no, Hunter definitely didn't like the sound of his voice, and followed Marks out of the hall like a naughty schoolboy. He'd just brought them an army, surely that proved he was still one of the good guys, surely they wouldn't damn him as a witch and therefore evil.

Outside it was bitterly cold with a bright sun. Little Hanting had never looked so idyllic on this sharp, clear day. The villagers were gone and the only movement was that of uniformed soldiers and their witch-hunter guides.

Anthony Marks stopped abruptly and turned to Hunter, his eyes blazing. When he spoke, his voice struggled to remain calm. "Well? Are you going to explain what the hell is going on? We're under serious threat from the Shadow Witch - a threat you've seemed to exacerbate, I might add - you disappear and your assistant refuses to say anything. A sergeant from the British Army materialises in the Manor and the Army is in the church hall. This all smacks of magic, Astley."

212

Hunter couldn't meet Marks' gaze, instead he looked vaguely over his shoulder.

"It's… complicated. Do you know what happens when a 7th gen witch-hunter is created? It turns out that we have evolved to be something more… gifted. Similar to the Benandanti, they were-"

"The Italian anti-witches, yes I know, get on with it," Marks interrupted harshly.

Hunter frowned. Christ, was he the only person not to have heard of them?

"I have some of their abilities, which I've used to bring in the army. We couldn't hope to win without their help. I know this sounds dodgy, but I'm not a witch and I'm still a witch-hunter, still the same guy. When this is all over we can debate the issue, but right now we don't have time. You just have to trust me."

Hunter watched Marks carefully, but the older witch-hunter gave nothing away with his stern expression.

"You were wrong to hide this from us, Astley." Marks eventually spoke, "How can we wage a war when you are going off on private jaunts with your own aims… What's left of the MMC could prosecute you on that alone. I knew your father, Young, he was a good man, and I'm sure you are too. Just promise me, no more secrets, no hidden agendas."

Hunter nodded. "I promise."

Marks took a deep breath and looked about the empty village. "Well I suppose we best form a council and go over the battle plan."

Without another word, Marks headed off. After a
moment or two, Hunter followed, not sure whether or
not he should be relieved.

Twenty-six

Everyone was on edge as they waited for the attack. But the short winter's day rolled on with no sign of activity. The soldiers and witch-hunters alike grumbled in the cold, and even Hunter began to doubt his assumption that Sophie would come for revenge, for him.

About 4 o' clock that afternoon, the sun dropped to the misty horizon and the world was half-lit in a grey light. Twilight.

"They're coming." Hunter breathed, his hand tightening about the cold handle of his gun

There was a suffocating silence, and a gentle breeze that was oddly warm. In the open space outside the village, figures began to appear, black and solid against the insubstantial evening. There was a throbbing pulse of magic that raised the head of every witch-hunter.

The witches were more than fifty in number, and they bristled with excitement as they marched behind their leader, the Shadow Witch. They came to the edge of the Astley estate and stopped, the magic of the

215

Manor doing its work. None could cross the invisible line without rendering themselves mortal.

In the privacy of every man and woman's mind, a voice echoed an ultimatum.

"Surrender and your lives shall be spared. All we demand is that you turn over Astley. Resist and you die."

Those inside the Manor exchanged grim looks. They did not sacrifice one of their own, nor did they compromise with witches. And upon feeling the hateful magic that brewed, none would trust their lives to the gathered witchkind.

Hunter gazed about the other witch-hunters that stood waiting in the hall for his signal. Their anxious faces lit by flickering firelight - at least they were warmer than those on patrol outside. James, Marks and twenty others, all silently relying on his questionable ability to protect them.

They might all die tonight. But there was no backing down.

Hunter took a deep breath and nodded, no point delaying the inevitable. The twenty fellow witch-hunters scrambled to their feet and followed him out of the warm Manor and into the cold, darkening evening. They marched over the flat ground, directed by that inner sense that detected magic.

There was a crowd of witches awaiting them, all charged with magic and excitement. They shifted so two opposing lines were formed, witches facing witch-hunters, just twenty feet apart, the Astley Estate border between them. The witches outnumbered the witch-hunters three times over.

The Shadow Witch stepped forward closer to the border. Her eyes immediately settled on Hunter. "You have come to give yourself up?"

Her question was answered by the tensing of the line and the metallic click of several guns readying.

"No, I didn't think you'd make it easy," the Shadow Witch said bitterly, a familiar frown creasing her beautiful features. "You can't win. Have your men lay down their weapons and they may live."

"Why don't you come over here and we'll discuss it," Hunter responded, stalling for time while others moved silently into position.

"I don't think so," Sophie replied. "Shall we see how the Astley protection stands up against the destructive power of the Shadow Witch?"

She raised her arms and there was the crackle of immense energy building up. Hunter suddenly saw in a flash the ruins and rubble of Brian Lloyd's house.

A gun discharged as one of the witch-hunters lost his nerve.

"NO!" Hunter barked, snapping back to the present.

The witches stood unfazed, apparently protected from something as insignificant as bullets.

"You can't win," Sophie repeated, her eyes unfocussed as she prepared to release her most destructive magic.

"You won't hurt anyone," Hunter whispered.

With those around him in danger, he let his desire to protect grow. It spread like a blanket over the witches and witch-hunters, regardless of borders. The Shadow Witch either couldn't feel it, or was too absorbed in her own spell to notice. She smiled and released her magic...

Nothing happened.

Sophie frowned, thinking it had been the power of the enchantments of the Manor that had stopped her. But it shouldn't be, she had lived there for months, she knew every defence and how to overcome it. Her eyes found Hunter again and her confusion turned to rage.

"ASTLEY! You utter bastard. How dare you... You weren't..." Sophie spat, her anger boiling over. "I warn you not to do this."

"Too late," Hunter replied quietly.

From the darkness, lines of soldiers and witch-hunters ran forward, aimed and fired.

The gathered witches laughed scornfully as the first shots rang out - for what could harm them in the presence of the Shadow Witch? But the laughter turned to screams of shock and fury and pain as the bullets ripped through, killing and maiming.

As one body, the witches turned to face their attackers, preparing to raise their reliable magic to destroy them. But again nothing happened, they were defenceless against the slaughter.

Sophie span, turned from one scene of tragedy to another as her loyal witches were shot down. They were surrounded, no escape on foot. Sophie tried, and failed, to raise her shadows to get the survivors out. Hunter, this was his doing. No bullet could penetrate her seething aura as she sought him.

Hunter stood firmly on Astley ground, using his Manor's enchantments for protection. Everyone else had gone forward to engage the enemy.

Hunter's eyes were open, but unseeing. He trembled in his stance as he struggled to maintain the block. He was starting to weaken, to slip, magic started to seep through the defences, he had to hold on.

He was vaguely aware of someone approaching. He was unsurprised that it should be Sophie.

"You shouldn't have told me... what I was," he gasped. "Your fault. It's your fault."

"Your magic shall die with you, Astley." Sophie spat, drawing closer, crossing the border that made her powerless.

Hunter shook his head with some difficulty. "You can't kill me."

Sophie hesitated. "Don't be so sure."

There was a flash of metal and movement. Hunter couldn't move fast enough to block the knife that drove into his torso. It felt cold, he realised, before the pain came.

He looked into Sophie's eyes, so close to his, and saw that her anger was gone, replaced by shock that drained the blood from her face.

Hunter felt the protective magic slip and fade, and he crumpled to the ground.

There was more gunfire, closer now. People continued to scream, but now others were calling his name.

It all grew fainter.

'What do you know, I was wrong,' he thought.

Then the world disappeared.

Twenty-seven

Hunter was lying somewhere warm, soft, and familiar. He was comfortable, so he stayed as he was while his mind caught up. Images of an army and a battle flashed behind his eyes, and somewhere the knowledge that he should be dead. Was he?

He was breathing, he could feel his heavy limbs, but not much more. He finally opened his eyes, squinting against the daylight. It looked like his bedroom in the Manor. He sighed, that wasn't his idea of heaven.

There was the sound of someone else in the room, alerted to his consciousness by the sigh.

"Hunter, you're awake. Thank god." The familiar voice was accompanied by a familiar figure hovering over him.

"James, you look terrible." Hunter said, his voice rough.

James grimaced, his face still bore the signs of torture at the hands of the witches. "Thanks mate, nice to see you too. Thought you were never gonna wake up."

"How long have I been out?"

"A couple of days," James replied.

Hunter frowned, then struggled to sit up, noticing the thick bandaging around his midriff and the odd, pain-free, sensation-free feeling. Which he guessed had plenty to do with copious amounts of morphine. Sitting up probably wasn't a good idea.

"What happened?" Hunter asked.

"Sophie stabbed you. You're lucky to be alive."

"I know that." Hunter grimaced. "But what happened in the fight? Sophie, was she..." killed? He couldn't bring himself to say the word.

"Sophie's gone. Not dead, as much as we tried. She ran and vanished. As for the rest, we'd eradicated most of the witches by the time you were attacked. Then there was nowhere for them to go, they were all eliminated, with surprisingly few casualties on our side," James filled in dutifully, still buoyed up on success.

Hunter sat quietly, taking it all in. They'd won, they had slaughtered their enemies. Never had Hunter been upset by the death of witches. So what had changed; was it because he was one? No matter how you phrased it he possessed magic. Or was it because... because he had loved one.

James, sensing that Hunter had a lot on his mind, made a weak excuse and left. Hunter hardly noticed him go, his thoughts were now on Sophie.

With no proof or reason, he had believed Bev when she said that Sophie could not kill him. Yet she had tried, she had meant to, it was only luck that had kept him alive.

Hunter remembered how pale Sophie had looked in that last moment, as if she were sharing his pain. Then she'd fled.

What came next was anyone's guess. Hunter could predict that he and Sophie would be the most hunted people by opposing parties. And neither could exist without seeking to destroy the other.

The future was dark and definitely interesting, and wholly full of possibilities.

And then the truth niggled away in a quiet corner of Hunter's thoughts and heart. He was in love with the woman that would kill him, and she was carrying his child.

Other books by K.S. Marsden:

Witch-Hunter
The Shadow Rises (Witch-Hunter #1)
> ➢ *Now available as audiobook*

The Shadow Reigns (Witch-Hunter #2)
The Shadow Falls (Witch-Hunter #3)

Witch-Hunter Prequels
James: Witch-Hunter (#0.5)
Kristen: Witch-Hunter (#2.5) ~ *avail only through* #Awethors
Sophie: Witch-Hunter (#0.5) ~ *coming soon*

Enchena
The Lost Soul: Book 1 of Enchena
The Oracle: Book 2 of Enchena

Northern Witch
Winter Trials (Northern Witch #1)
Awaken (Northern Witch #2)

If you enjoyed **The Shadow Rises**, read on for a sneak peak of The Shadow Reigns…

An insight from our villain

For hundreds of years witches have been persecuted; forced to keep their heads down and conform to laws that we never agreed to. To be a witch is to live a hunted life; to suffer the stupidity and ignorance of those around you, even though you could outclass them with the simplest spell.

I was born to free the witches from oppression. I am the Shadow Witch. I have freed my kin from the so-called justice of the witch-hunters and their Malleus Maleficarum Council. In one night, the world was thrown into chaos, and for once it was the witch-hunters that were forced back.

We followed our victory with a second. We pitched the world into darkness, and removed the advantage technology gave our enemies. The new world has already begun, and in this spiralling darkness, those with magic will finally be able to rise above all others.

Then why do I feel guilt? Why do I feel doubt?

Ever since the witches told me of my destiny, when I was thirteen and powerless, I have never felt any doubt in my path. When my powers were awakened seven years later – the witches conducting sacrifices on Hallowe'en to break the ancient spell holding them back – I was even more sure of what lay ahead.

But it is shallow of me to even pretend I do not know the reason that I finally question everything.

Him. For years I hated the very name Astley, knowing that they were the witch-hunters that killed Sara Murray, the last Shadow Witch; and all its consequences. I would not be the same if she lived; I would not have to take up this brutal destiny.

I had not planned to fall in love with the current bearer of the name: George "Hunter" Astley. I ignored the attraction at first; whenever he was around I told myself it was the excitement of playing him for a fool that thrilled me so, not his presence itself. But after months of secretly savouring each glance, each touch, I wanted more. I knew from the beginning that our relationship was doomed; I could not stay with him and soon we would be on the opposite sides of a war. Is it wrong I tried to find a way to keep him with me? If not for my sake, then for our child's?

Not that it mattered. In the end he chose his side, and I chose mine.

I knew that I was expected to kill him when we met again, and I was prepared to do so. I came so close and failed. As my knife got past his guard and cut deep into him, I felt a shock of pain stab through me. It was all I could do to evade his witch-hunters and return home, where I collapsed at my mother's feet.

I have been recovering slowly for a month now. I cannot explain it, there is no physical wound; I can only guess that what was inflicted on him rebounded to me. None of the witches can explain why, but some theorise that the child links us – we can only guess what powers he or she shall inherit. In which case, if this is true; I shall withdraw as much as possible until it is born, and hope the spell breaks.

One

Little Hanting was a picturesque village in the English countryside. Quaint bungalows and farmhouses fanned out from the church hall, with its perfectly manicured green in front of it. Not that the grass could be seen; fresh snow had again fallen the previous night, coating everything with a perfect whiteness. All it needed was children with mittens having a snowball fight, and the scene would be idyllic.

But Little Hanting silently suffered. The inhabitants had all been evacuated when the village had been the setting for a decisive battle. Now all the homes lay eerily quiet, save for the ones that had been temporarily taken over by soldiers. They sheltered from the cold and waited – waited for answers and for their next move. They would huddle around the fireplaces, casting glances in the direction of the local manor house.

*****

Hunter drifted in a haze of painkillers and nightmares. He saw the flash of the knife a hundred times, Sophie's hazel eyes, and the pain that tore through them both.

The scene would change, and it was Hunter's first day at University, and Brian was coming to tell him that his father was dead. Charlotte should be here to comfort him. Where was Charlotte?

229

When Hunter was awake... lucid was hardly applicable. He lay in his bed, staring at the high ceiling, with all its familiar cracks. Or he would turn his head to observe the dark drapes that someone opened and closed with the passing of day and night. Huh, probably the same someone that fed the fire in his bedroom to stop it being too cold.

Not that Hunter cared, the cold was numbing, and combined with the morphine, opium – whatever drug they managed to dredge up, it was a good haze. It stopped him having to think as much. Or at least, it kept his thoughts strangely disconnected from himself.

So this was what it was like to wallow. Hunter had never been much of a wallower: not when the witches had killed his father; Brian; Charlotte... Hunter was a witch-hunter, as they all had been. It was accepted as fact that you would lose friends and family, that you yourself would be a target. To be a part of the Malleus Maleficarum Council, to protect the people from the violence of witches was to invite that violence onto oneself.

But the pain of the past was nothing compared to what he was putting off feeling now. It wasn't as if Sophie had died – although Hunter wished she had. No, it had been worse. The woman he loved had turned out to be the Shadow Witch. It sickened him to think of the nights spent together, the caresses, the half-asleep conversations. And the days when he had never doubted his trust in her as a colleague and a friend. How could she have acted so innocently and seemed so honest when she had just killed his old mentor and closest friend?

Before, grief had only driven him harder to fight back against witches. Now Hunter felt confusion over his life's work in eradicating witches. He had fallen in love with one, and now she carried his child; and Hunter had recently discovered his own magic-like abilities.

Hunter had thought Sophie mad, and looking for a loophole when she had sworn that he was different from his fellow witch-hunters.

It was something that Hunter, and every MMC worldwide took for granted that, in a family of witch-hunters, each generation would become more adept. By the 3rd gen they could perceive spells being cast, and were immune to some magic; as well as being stronger and faster. As an unheard of 7th gen, Hunter Astley had been revered by the MMC. How little everyone (including himself) knew that he would evolve into a magic-wielder.

Which left him with the question: should he use his new talents in this war; or should he copy the fabled Benandanti and kill himself for being a witch?

He had no answers, and the thoughts just swirled incessantly in his head while he tried to numb them.

The only thing that broke the cycle of monotonous thought was mealtimes. Usually someone left a coffee on his bedside table in a morning, although chances were that it would still be sitting there, stone-cold, by midday. And then someone would bring him some lunch.

This irritating someone came in the form of Hunter's best friend, James Bennett. He was a pretty average guy – average height, average brown hair and eyes. He was a little more intelligent than most. But this 1st gen witch-hunter was the truest and bravest person that Hunter knew. Oh, and James also had an invaluable knack for putting up with Hunter on a daily basis. Hunter couldn't remember a time when James hadn't been there for him.

Which included bringing him meals while Hunter was injured, it seemed. Hunter was never very hungry, and would have left the unappetising food if James hadn't stayed. Not that James was watching and making sure his friend actually ate something. No, it just so happened that mealtimes coincided with James having found something interesting in the Astley library, and brought up one old book or another to get Hunter's opinion.

Twice a day. Every day.

Today was a little different. James sat with the typical book on his lap, and the non-typical red pointy hat on his head.

Hunter shot him a few looks, but today James was staying quiet. Hunter dutifully finished his soup and the last of the bread, pointedly putting the bowl aside to state it was empty.

"Why?" Hunter asked simply.

"Why what?" James returned innocently, looking up from his book.

Hunter sighed. "The hat?"

"Oh, that. I thought it'd annoy your mum." James replied with a shrug. "And it's my birthday. One of the soldiers found this and thought it wa' funny."

That made Hunter sit up and pay attention. "What? It's the end of January already? Oh shit, I'm sorry James, I forgot. It's just... it's been a blur, I lost track."

James shrugged again, but Hunter noticed the mischievous glint in his eye. "Hey, it's fine. We've all been preoccupied with somethin' a bit bigger than my birthday. Besides, I distinctly remember you saying that if you forgot my birthday, I could have that bottle of '82 Chateau Gruard Larose that's in your cellar."

"Oh, I said that, did I?" Hunter tried to keep a straight face.

"Yep, absolutely." James replied sincerely, pushing the reading glasses back up his nose.

"Ok, so I get the hat. What's with the glasses?"

James looked a little surprised at the question. "Dunno, I just find it easier reading with them. Maybe the witches did some damage when they beat the crap out of me. Or maybe I should just admit I'm getting old."

Hunter snorted. "Twenty-five is not old. Oh, sorry, twenty-six now. Happy Birthday."

"I thought they made me look more intelligent." James continued.

"Well you couldn't look any less so." Hunter returned quickly.

James looked ready to throw his book at him, but seemed to think better of it. Instead, he got to his feet.

"Well, you seem back on form, Hunter. So perhaps you'll think about getting your arse out of bed. We've a war to plan. And we could do with your help in keeping Mrs Astley in check."

Hunter groaned, more at the mention of his mother than impending war.

"And you might want to shave." James added, eyeing the scruffy attempt of a beard his face was sporting. "Or not. I could be the handsome one, as well as the smart one."

With a chuckle, James turned and finally left.

Two

Hunter finally made it downstairs that afternoon, cleaned up, dressed, and looking much more his old self. The beard was gone, and his black hair combed into something resembling control. He'd managed to find a clean jumper and jeans, and looked presentable.

He was greeted by a warm chorus from a crowd of people in what used to be the dining room. Astley Manor had been in his family for nearly two hundred years; the image of extravagant Georgian architecture, it was comfort and luxury for the line of Astley witch-hunters. And the house had its own secrets, no witch could enter the Manor without their powers being stripped; no magic could be used in the extensive estate. The only exception being Hunter's anti-magic talents.

Which made it the perfect emergency home for the Malleus Maleficarum Council after the witches had destroyed their base. After their initial defeat, witch-hunters had trickled into Astley Manor, seeking safety, and planning their next attack.

Hunter was more than happy to open his home to his allies, but even the vast Astley Manor was not big enough to house them all, especially after the additional influx of soldiers for the last battle. Those that could not be made comfortable in the Manor stayed in the village, and travelled in every day to learn of any progress made.

The over-crowding of the Manor was not universally welcomed. One in particular loathed it - Mrs Astley. Hunter's mother had always had very strict rules over protocol and etiquette, and this flooding of the Manor with allsorts insulted her deeply. The last straw was the dining room. After the witch-hunter hooligans converted that into a war room, Mrs Astley resigned to her rooms and refused to come out unless absolutely necessary.

At this very moment, about a dozen people sat around the large table, most of them nursing a fresh mug of tea. The two most senior stood up at Hunter's appearance.

"Mr Astley, it's good to see you up and about." General Hayworth smiled as he looked over Hunter, a touch of concern in his blue eyes.

"Thank you, General." Hunter replied, trying to hide how breathless he was from just coming downstairs. "My nurse has cleared me for duty again."

"Huh. Well, sit down before you fall down, Astley." 5th gen Anthony Marks said with a shake of his head.

Hunter smiled bitterly, embarrassed at how weak his body had become. He obediently took an empty seat and looked expectantly towards the two older men. "So, can you bring me up-to-date?"

General Hayworth returned to his chair and started first. "It's been three weeks since the battle, the witches must know about it by now and are giving us a wide berth. Communications are still down, so it's hard to get any real idea of what they're doing at this time. They are probably doing the same as us – assessing the situation and strengthening their forces."

"And how are our forces?"

Anthony Marks sighed. "Again, with no way of getting in touch quickly, we can only guess. Aside from the forty-seven witch-hunters that were in the battle, we've had others making their way here over the weeks. There's nearly a hundred now. We've housed them in Little Hanting alongside the soldiers. We have been sending out patrols to try and find more, but it's a slow process."

"This lack of technology is a pain in the arse." Hayworth interjected.

"That would be why they did it." Hunter muttered. He remembered Sophie gloating over the blanket of magic that disrupted most technology. Hunter and his colleagues had been thrown back into the dark ages, while Sophie and her witches had their magic to get by and make faster progress.

Marks frowned at Hunter's comment, but brushed over it. "We've started sourcing generators, most of them are in working condition, we've just got to keep an eye on fuel usage. Luckily the Manor was built before our dependency on technology, so no problems here. As for the MMC... the Council is destroyed. As the most senior member, I have officially assumed control. Until someone more senior steps up, of course."

Hunter grew uncomfortable under Marks' steady gaze. It was crazy – Anthony Marks was twice Hunter's age; Hunter had grown up hearing nothing but positive accounts of this witch-hunter from both his father and his trainer, Brian Lloyd. But because Hunter had been born an unheard of 7th gen, that automatically gave him superiority. All he had to do was claim it.

"I'm not going to do that, Mr Marks. I never wanted to lead."

General Hayworth chuckled at his comment. "Who the hell does want to take responsibility and lead? Especially now the world's screwed up." He looked over at Marks. "Looks like you're stuck with the gig, Anthony. Now, pay up."

Sighing, Anthony shifted in his seat and pulled a crumpled note out of his pocket, handing it reluctantly to Hayworth. Around the table there were a few more subtle exchanges.

"We had a little wager going on. Had to amuse ourselves somehow, waiting for you to pop up again." Hayworth grinned as he explained to Hunter.

Hunter wasn't sure how he felt about this amusement at his expense, but he let it slide. "I wouldn't trust myself to make the right decisions. I'm too close to this."

The room fell silent, and Hunter wondered how much these men knew. James knew everything, having gone right through it all with Hunter. The General knew an edited version that Hunter had shared with him before the battle, but how much more had he learnt? And how much did the others know, or guess?

"Fine." Marks finally said. "Well as your Head of Council, I need to know how soon you can start that travelling in a blink again. It would be a monumental advantage to have you cover so much ground. It'd also mean we can save our fuel rations for something more important."

Hunter stared down at the table, his 'blinking' still felt like a dirty secret. But at least these guys weren't preparing to burn him at the stake. Yet. "I need to build my strength again. I will keep you informed on my progress, sir."

"Good. You go do that. And, ah…" Marks pulled a face, which told Hunter exactly what he was going to bring up next. "Perhaps you should go see if you can placate your mother. She doesn't seem too chuffed to have us here."

Hunter nodded and, finding no reasonable excuse for putting it off until later, he promptly made his way to his mother's rooms.

Mrs Astley had a whole wing to herself, with a bedroom, office, drawing room and a large bathroom all for her private use. She liked having the space to herself, especially when her son insisted on bringing all sorts of waifs and strays to stay. Her space was even more important to her now that her home had been invaded and militarised.

Hunter rarely came to this part of the house. His mother was not his favourite person, he'd had very few reasons over the years to seek out her company. Especially as Mrs Astley would often pop up and interfere, whether she was welcome, or not.

Hunter turned the handle to her main room, pushing the door open and giving it a couple of sharp knocks to announce his presence. He walked into the expensively-furnished drawing room, looking for his mad ol- dear, loving mother.

"Mother?" He called out.

"George, how many times must I tell you that it is common decency to wait for permission to enter." The familiar sharp tones snapped.

Hunter turned to see his mother, and their butler Charles, sitting by the window, playing chess.

"One of these days you will walk in while I am indisposed, and I daresay the embarrassment will be punishment enough." Mrs Astley added, her fingers

240

hovering over a black rook, then finally making her move.

"I'm sorry, mother. I won't do it again." Hunter replied, wincing slightly at the image she provided.

"Of course you'll do it again, you never learn from your mistakes – just like your father."

Ah yes, there it was. Hunter wondered if they could make it through a single conversation without his mother bringing up George "Young" Astley. Hunter worshipped the memory of his late father. His mother still blamed Young for ruining her life. She often wished he had left her to be sacrificed by witches, rather than give her this life. How many times had Hunter heard that over the years?

"I haven't seen you for a month, why have you been avoiding me this time?" Mrs Astley cut through her son's train of thought.

Hunter stared at her, wondering if she was really so ignorant to everything going on around her. "Mother, I've been an invalid. Laid up in bed for three weeks, recovering after Sophie tried to kill me."

"Oh." Mrs Astley finally looked away from her chess game to see her son. Her eyes ran quickly from head to toe, but seeing no real problem, she finally met his gaze. "Sophie, that common girl you were dating? Well, I did tell you not to bother with her."

Hunter clenched his fists and tried not to show how much his mother was winding him up right now. She told him not to bother with Sophie? Oh, so somehow Mrs Astley could tell that Sophie was evil, and the biggest threat this century? No, more likely the stuck-up Mrs Astley was offended by her son's interest in a "common" girl.

Mrs Astley sighed, reading her son's reaction. One that did not need an audience. "Charles, more tea."

The ever-dutiful Charles nodded, and stood up from the chess game, more than happy to leave the Astleys to yet another family interlude.

Once the butler had gone, Hunter drifted over to the table and chessboard that were set by the window, to get the most of the winter sun. He could see that Charles' white pieces could checkmate his mother in three moves. It wouldn't happen of course, Charles always let Mrs Astley win.

"Don't look at the board pretending you know how to play chess, George." Mrs Astley snapped.

"I do know how to play chess, mother. James taught me years ago." Hunter replied calmly.

"Oh, don't mention that odious boy!" Mrs Astley fumed, something about the Yorkshireman always seemed to rile her up. "He is still staying here, I presume? You should start charging him rent."

"Mother… things have changed. Witch-hunters need somewhere safe to stay." Hunter said, trying to change her way of looking at it.

"And that Marks fellow – running around like he owns this place! I imagine he always had his beady eye on the Manor, when he used to come visit Young. Now he goes and fills it with all sorts!"

Hunter waited impatiently for his mother's rant to end. "No mother, I own this place. And as lord of Astley Manor, I turned it into a centre of control for the MMC, I have encouraged witch-hunters to use it as a sanctuary. And I pushed Anthony Marks to take command."

Mrs Astley sat thin-lipped, considering this. "I am not sharing my rooms." She eventually announced.

"No one is asking you to, mother." Hunter replied with a touch of exasperation. "They are being housed in the village too, there's space enough."

"What?" Mrs Astley looked up at her son with surprise. "The villagers will not take kindly to you pushing house guests on them."

Hunter narrowed his eyes at his mother. "The villagers were evacuated three weeks ago to save them from the witches."

"Oh." Mrs Astley took this bit of news in. "So that must be why Mrs Harsmith has not been to visit. I assumed she had the flu again."

Hunter was caught at that familiar place between wanting to laugh at her, and being thoroughly annoyed by her. He decided to take the safest path.

"I will leave you to your tea and chess, mother."